PRIVATE CHARTER

N.R. WALKER

DEDICATION

For anyone who needs reminding.
Life is short, live your dream.

BLURB

Stuart Jenner's job is high stress, high stakes, and everything he's strived for. So why, when the apex of his career is within reach, does he stumble? At his doctor's insistence, he books a privately chartered yacht to sail around the tropics for two weeks of sun, surf, and sex. When his friend-with-benefits bails on him at the last minute, Stuart decides to go alone.

Foster Knight left the rat race behind six years ago, bought a yacht, and now calls the Great Barrier Reef his home. Sailing tourists around tropical waters is all in a day's work, and he's never been happier. When his next client arrives alone, the two-week charter will be the most private job he's ever had.

Foster can see how stressed and exhausted Stuart is, and he promises him extensive rest and relaxation. Stuart slowly realises his original plan for two weeks of sun, surf, and sex might not be lost yet. Confined to a yacht, isolated by aqua-coloured oceans and the sweltering sun, Stuart and Foster are about to find out just how hot the tropics can get.

COPYRIGHT

Author's Note:

While care for the finer details of sailing have been taken, there have been some liberties as well. Enjoy!

PRIVATE
Charter

N. R. WALKER

CHAPTER ONE

STUART JENNER

I NEEDED THIS. I was burnt out. Stressed, exhausted. My mind was no better than mush. I'd busted my arse to close my last deal, and at six twenty-five on Friday afternoon, I walked out of my office pumped for my much-needed holiday.

Twelve days of sun, surf, sailing, swimming, and a whole lot of sex.

I pulled out my phone with every intention of calling Jason, but it rang in my hand. My boss's name flashed up on screen. *Gerard Soto.* I wasn't even out of the damn building. I gritted my teeth and hit Answer. "You've reached the answering machine of Stuart Jenner. Please leave a message."

"Nice try, Jenner."

I rolled my eyes, but I stopped walking. If he needed to see me, I'd only have to turn around and go back. And, as much as I hated it, we both knew I would. "Boss. What can I do for you?"

"Signed off on the Goodridge account?"

"Of course I did."

"And the Washington prelims?"

"Contract's with legal. I hand delivered it to Browning myself."

"Mmm" was his only response. Then, "And I assume your full monthly report is on my desk."

A full month report for half of which I wouldn't be there. "Of course it is."

There was a reason I was one of the best corporate finance senior analysts in Brisbane. So good, in fact, that when headhunters from Sydney and Singapore tried to lure me away, my boss offered me an incredibly lucrative offer to stay. Stay I did, which is why he now owned me. So when he called, I answered. When he asked, I delivered.

I had no doubt he knew the report was filed before he even asked. Soto played little egomaniac games like that. "What time are you leaving tomorrow?"

He was really asking how late he could call me. I unclenched my jaw and put a smile on my face, even though he couldn't see it. "My flight leaves at six thirty tomorrow morning." I looked at my watch. Twelve hours.

"And you won't be contactable?" he asked. Again.

"No. No phone service, no internet." That wasn't technically true. I would have some limited access, but he didn't know that. "There will be a satellite phone for emergencies. I can get you the number if you need."

"Mmm, no, that won't be necessary," he added flatly. I only offered because I knew damn well he wouldn't want to call a satellite phone for what was no doubt a menial question. "Well, then…"

"Okay, I'll see you on the twenty-seventh."

"Right. Yes. I suppose I should wish you a good vacation."

I almost laughed at his compassion. "Thank you."

"Come back well-rested."

That sounded almost like a threat.

"That's the plan."

He mumbled something that sounded like a goodbye, and the line went dead. I took a few deep breaths, trying to keep my blood pressure in check, though the thumping in my temples told me it was pointless. I kept my phone in my hand, slung my messenger bag over my shoulder, and took the elevator down to the basement car park. The heat and humidity of Brisbane in February weren't particularly pleasant in a suit, but I didn't care.

I had two weeks off. Two whole weeks.

Two weeks at my doctor's insistence, but a holiday nonetheless.

Overworked, over-stressed, and over the rat race, that's what I was. I was thirty-four and headed for a massive heart attack, she'd warned. "You need a break, and you need one now."

I took the vacation time but left out the medical push behind it. Gerard Soto didn't need to know his golden boy was starting to show fault lines. Or maybe stress fractures would be a more apt description.

I slid in behind the wheel of my car, popped my phone into its cradle, and started the engine. As soon as I was out of the car park and away from layers of concrete and steel, I hit Bluetooth. "Call Jason."

His number came up and it rang, and rang, and rang. I hit End Call before it went through to his voice mail. Maybe he was stuck at work or at the gym or in the shower... Hopefully he was already packed to leave and on his way to my place.

I tried him again as I stepped out of the elevator at my apartment, and again, no answer.

Great.

I smiled at my packed bag as I tore off my suit and, deciding on a cool shower, let the water wash away the shitty day. And as I dressed in some casual shorts and a T-shirt, I was already in holiday mode.

The original plan was for me to pick Jason up before heading to the airport in the morning, but I wondered if he might like to stay here tonight. We could order in his favourite Chinese, watch a movie, go to bed early...

If he would answer his damn phone.

I tried again, still no answer. My plans for a relaxing, easy night for two became a sad and lonely night for one. I rummaged around my kitchen to make myself some dinner; I'd not ordered any new groceries because I was going away, and I couldn't be arsed ordering in for one, so I settled on a very depressing bowl of cereal for dinner. Nothing on TV held my interest, and after I spent an hour flicking back and forth through stupid channels, I sent Jason a text.

Pick you up at 5am. Be out the front. Need me to send you a wake-up call?

I smiled as I hit Send. He was never fully operational at that time of day.

A bubble appeared, signalling he was replying. Then it disappeared, then reappeared, then disappeared, and I was frowning at my phone when it rang. It was Jason, and I knew this wasn't going to be a good phone call.

"Hey," he started. "Um."

"Just say it, Jason," I said, not caring to keep the bite from my tone. It was crazy how easily I could slip into professional shark mode. All business and zero tolerance for bullshit.

Music played and people talked in the background. So he was out somewhere, and he had absolutely no intention of coming with me tomorrow. Now I wondered if he'd ever intended to come with me in the first place.

"Well, you see," he said, "I can't go. Something came up at work and I only found out yesterday. I tried sorting it out today so I could get away, but you know how these things go."

The funny thing is, I *did* know. We worked in the same industry. I knew exactly how it went. I also knew exactly how Jason operated. "Well, I hope he's worth it."

There was a muffled sound followed by his silence, though the music still played. "It's not really like that."

"I get it," I said coolly. "Next time someone offers you an all-expenses-paid two-week holiday, try giving them some notice so they can replace you. Because you are replaceable." I could have asked any of my casual hook-ups if they wanted to come with me. Jason was normally fun to hang with and we got on okay. Though we'd rarely spent more than one night together at any given time, and maybe two weeks alone on a sailboat would be a bit much, but dammit, he could have said no when I asked.

"Yeah, I'm sorry, but work—"

"It's fine. I'll see you around."

I didn't wait for his reply. I ended the call and threw my phone on the coffee table. Fuck, fuck, fuck.

I wasn't ringing around my hook-up list to ask if any of them could get two weeks off work and oh, by the way, we're leaving at six o'clock tomorrow morning...

Fuck.

Well, that just took the 'whole lotta sex' out of the sun, sailing, swimming equation I had planned for my holiday.

Right, then. I considered taking the two boxes of condoms out—because what was the point?—but decided to keep them. With a bit of luck, when we docked into port at a few of the holiday towns, there might be some nightclubs. I considered googling the gay bar scene in Far North Queensland, but I'd just thrown my phone across the coffee table and I couldn't be arsed getting up.

Fuck Jason for messing me around and for ruining my holiday before it even began.

It was settled. I was going on a hired yacht for two weeks around the Great Barrier Reef in tropical North Queensland by myself. Just me and the skipper. If he was some crusty old dude who never shut up, I'd just throw myself overboard. Or if it was some middle-aged woman who never shut up, I'd throw myself overboard. Or maybe pretending to suffer chronic seasickness and needing to fly home would be less dramatic. At least the skipper was LGBT friendly—they advertised as such—so that was one less worry.

But goddammit. I was going on this holiday, and I was going to lie in the fucking sun and relax. I just hoped the skipper of the yacht was a nice person, because for the next twelve days, twenty-four hours a day, it was just going to be nothing but me, them, and a whole lotta ocean.

CHAPTER TWO

FOSTER KNIGHT

I HAD enough supplies to last three people three days, before we would need to restock somewhere up the coast. This job was a two-weeker for one couple. When the bookings came in, if the couples' names indicated they were two men or two women, the head office usually booked them with me.

Being gay myself, I didn't mind the guys getting it on in front of me, and lesbian couples usually preferred my orientation. Less threatening than a straight guy who might want in on the action, I guessed.

Because when we're miles off the coast surrounded by nothing but water for days at a time, the customers needed to be comfortable around me, and not just confident in my ability to sail, but also to leave them alone.

My yacht was only fourteen metres, or forty-five feet, long. There were three cabins and one communal lounge space, galley, and bathroom. There wasn't a great deal of room to hide from one another, and I did get to know my clients quite well. I was always excited to meet my new clients, and usually within the first five minutes of meeting them, I knew what they needed me to be. If they wanted a vocal coastal guide, a storyteller with a funny yarn to make them laugh, or if they needed me to be seen and not heard.

So I was surprised when I stood at the marina entrance, waiting for two guys to turn up, that the only guy to arrive, seeming out of place and like he was looking for someone, was on his own.

"Are you looking for Tropic Heat Tours?" I asked.

He stopped, looked at me, and did a double take. "Uh, yeah. I think that's it."

"Stuart Jenner and Jason Hardgrave? Party of two?" I asked, hoping to clarify.

He smiled and extended his hand. "Stuart Jenner. Now a party of one. Is that okay?"

Oh. One? "Yeah, sure, that's perfectly fine." I took his duffle bag and shook his hand. "Foster Knight." I gestured to the jetty and we headed toward it. "Everything okay with your friend?"

"The short version is he's not coming," he snapped.

Right then. Jesus. This was going to be an interesting and more than likely awkward two weeks if this guy was going to be an arsehole the entire time.

He sighed and his shoulders fell. "Sorry. It's been a... I'm sorry. He decided to tell me last night he wasn't coming."

I looked at him as we walked toward the end of the jetty. He wore khaki shorts and a light blue button-down, short-sleeve shirt. He had brown hair, short back and sides, dark brown eyes, and a jaw that could cut glass. But he also had dark circles under his eyes and looked like he hadn't slept in years. He squinted at the sunshine, and I was reminded he'd broken up with his boyfriend last night and been up since God knew when. Or maybe he hadn't sleep at all. "That's okay. No apology needed," I said, giving him my best smile. "How was your flight here? You're from..."

"Brisbane," he answered. "Flight was okay. Non-eventful, which is always good. Can I tell you that I am so looking forward to this holiday? Like you can't believe."

I stopped walking, and he did too. "Well, I hope it's everything you want it to be."

"Sun, sleep, swimming, sailing, seafood," he replied. Jesus, he really did look exhausted.

"Then you've come to the right place." I turned to my pride and joy. My home. "This is her."

My yacht was a Beneteau Oceanis 45. She was sleek and streamlined, white with dark tinted windows, and her rear deck was whitewashed wooden slats. The name, White Knight, was painted on the back, and the abstract outline of a knight's profile finished the design.

Everyone assumed the Knight reference was to my name, and it was, mostly. I never bothered explaining the play on words, not that anyone ever asked.

"Home for the next twelve days," I said, stepping aboard. "Come on, I'll show you to your quarters."

He followed, taking in my yacht. His wide eyes and smile told me he liked what he saw. "Wow. The photos don't do it justice," he said as we climbed down the stairs into the cabin.

I gestured toward the lounge seating area, then to the galley. "Fully stocked fridge and pantry. Help yourself to anything at any time. I'll be your chef extraordinaire. You pre-selected your menu, but we can change it up a bit if you want. It'll just be you and me, so whatever you want. Just ask."

He nodded slowly. "I suppose you ordered enough food

for two clients. Sorry about that."

I waved him off. "It's no problem. Means more beer for you." He clearly was feeling pretty down, so I grinned at him. "More everything for us. But we're scheduled to dock at a few marinas up and down the coast, so if you want anything else, just let me know and I'll grab it for you. Nothing's a problem."

"Okay, thanks," he mumbled distractedly, looking around the interior. "It's beautiful."

I loved people's first impression. It never got old. "She sure is." I showed him the bathroom, then opened the door to the master cabin at the bow of the boat. "This is your room. You have your own en-suite."

He poked his head into the room. "Is this the biggest one?"

"Yes. Not huge, but you are on a yacht, not in a hotel." I tried to keep my tone light, but was he really put out with the size of the room?

"Oh, no," he said quickly. "I just assumed you'd have the biggest room."

Oh.

"Customer first, right? I have the room on the aft port side," I explained, pointing back to one of the two rooms near the ladder. "I don't need much. I'd prefer you to be comfortable."

He stepped into his cabin and put his bag on the bed. He took the whole room in and seemed to sag a little. "Well, this is great, thank you."

"Why don't you get settled in. Maybe even take a nap. I'll be taking us out through the harbour going south at first, and it's always slow going until we hit open water."

"Slow going?"

"Oh, sure. There's a major sugar export terminal, an operational naval base, customs and water police depots, commercial fishing fleet, slipways and floating docks, shipping companies, fishing and diving tour companies..."

"Oh." He laughed. "I didn't realise it was so busy."

I gave him a smile. "You good?"

He smiled back, tired, but the way his lips curved crookedly gave his hard face a softer edge. "Yeah, I'm good. But I am kind of tired," he mumbled, playing absentmindedly with the strap of his bag as he looked at the bed.

"Then I'll leave you to it," I replied, doing exactly that. I went back up on deck, and kicked the engine over. She purred to life, I pulled in the dock lines, and pushed off from the jetty then slowly took us out of Marlin Marina.

The port was busy, but I poked along, taking my time to get outside the harbour. I loved this part of my job; just me in the cockpit and nothing else but the blue sky and aqua-coloured ocean. I'd travelled all over the world, but nowhere else compared to the tropics of North Queensland, the Whitsundays, and the Barrier Reef.

But what I really loved, like *really* loved, was when I could hoist the sails, kill the engine, and sail.

That was where my heart was. Being taken on the wind at the mercy of Mother Nature and the elements she commanded.

I loved the power of it, challenging the force of it. It would never get old. Ever.

I'd held corporate power before. I'd known that rush, that addiction. That soul-sucking, life-crushing vacuum. But this was power and freedom, and that was the biggest rush for me. And I'd never felt more alive.

I took us south as I said I would, only at half pace, around to the bottom of Fitzroy Island, and kept a steady pace down the coast. My schedule didn't call for rushing anymore, and the only references to time I kept my eye on these days were the sun and the moon and tide charts. The only deadlines I had to meet were my own. If we got to our first stop today or tomorrow was neither here nor there. I had almost two weeks to show Stuart around the Whitsundays.

And as he slept below, I had to wonder what his story was. He'd arrived alone, and it was pretty clear it wasn't his choice to do so. He was a good-looking guy; I couldn't deny that. I just hoped these two weeks together weren't awkward. I'd never done a one-on-one before. I had no idea what his expectations were, or his intentions.

But he was exhausted, I could see that much. So, once we were well clear of other vessels and without knowing how long he might nap, I let us heave to, which was sail-speak for taking a break. I sat at the wheel, one foot up on the side, and leaned back, breathing in deep lungfuls of salt air and letting the sounds of the ocean wash around me. Gulls sounded overhead and water lapped at the hull. It was a symphony behind the silence, and I could listen to it all day.

But morning would soon be afternoon, and still, Stuart hadn't come out. I wasn't sure if he was avoiding me, or maybe he found the fact it was just the two of us beyond awkward. But there was one sure way to get him out of his cabin without blatantly knocking.

I fired up the grill.

While the king prawns cooked, I diced up some mangoes and avocado and added some dressing with just enough chilli to make your lips tingle. And sure enough, just as I was plating up, his cabin door opened and a sleep-rumpled Stuart appeared.

"Oh, perfect timing," I said with a smile, handing him a plate.

He took his lunch and scrunched his face up in that still-half-asleep way and shook it off. "Sorry. Thought I'd just snooze for a bit. Didn't mean to fall asleep like that."

"It's all good." I handed him a fork. "You haven't missed much. I slowed us right down. I didn't want to sail right past anything you might've wanted to see."

I took two bottled waters from the fridge, tucked them under arm, collected my plate, and climbed the stairs to the cockpit. Stuart followed, and when he was up top, he looked around at the vastness of blue-green ocean to the starboard side and the gorgeous forested coastline, and he smiled. "Wow."

I laughed and took my seat at the wheel, and he joined me on the long bench seat that spanned the width of the cockpit. The sun was bright and warm, the wind was a cool relief. "Not a bad view, huh?"

"Do you ever get sick of it?"

"Never."

He smiled at that and bit into a prawn. "Oh my God. Did you just cook this?"

"Two minutes ago." I took another mouthful and smiled as I chewed. Most people had the same reaction.

"It's amazing."

"It's fresh prawns, caught this morning, and my aunt's tropical salsa and dressing recipe. Takes all of three minutes."

He waved his fork in the air while he chewed and swallowed. "Well, thank your aunt for me. This is heavenly."

I chuckled. "I will. She'll be pleased."

He ate another bite and sighed, closing his eyes to the sunshine, and just enjoyed the warmth and the breeze and repeated this until his plate was empty. I could see him relax a fraction with every sigh, with every second he took to just breathe.

"Sleep okay?"

"So good," he answered without opening his eyes. His head was back, his face basking in the sunshine, and it allowed me the opportunity to study him without being noticed. Yes, he really was good-looking. His jawline was an angle I could have measured with a set square. "Seriously, that bed and the rocking of the boat, and I was out like a light."

I chuckled. "Yeah, it's not bad."

He cracked one eye open. "So you sail the tropics for a living and you can cook like a chef, and people pay you a small fortune. Do you have the world's best job?"

I grinned at him. "I think so. Others might disagree."

He closed his eyes and smiled. "Others would be wrong."

"Here, let me take your plate," I said, standing up. He looked at me long enough to hand it over but soon closed his eyes again.

"I don't know whether it's best to bask in the sunshine or to take in the view," he murmured.

"Both usually works," I offered, disappearing below deck. It only took me a minute to load everything into the dishwasher, and when I went back on deck, he hadn't moved. His legs were outstretched, crossed at the ankles, his arms resting on the back-rest, his eyes still closed. He certainly wasn't difficult to look at, and he seemed so much more agreeable now he'd rested a bit. Maybe even friendly. That crooked smile looked good on him.

I took my seat behind the wheel next to him and he slowly opened his eyes. "What's on the agenda for this afternoon?"

"Much of the same, if that's okay."

"Very okay."

"There's an inlet with a small beach a few miles up that's usually secluded. We can anchor there and swim if you want."

"Sounds perfect to me."

"Well, I'm completely at your beck and call," I added. "I've never done a one-on-one job before."

He met my gaze and didn't look away. "Does it make you uncomfortable?"

He clearly had nerves of steel to look someone right in the eyes and ask them questions that could make things awkward. I got the feeling he used the same tactic to gain the upper hand in boardrooms or business meetings. I used to do the same thing. I stared right back at him, a smile tugging at my lips. "Not at all. Sorry your boyfriend bailed out though."

He didn't look away. "He wasn't my boyfriend. Just an occasional acquaintance, if you get my meaning." He sighed dramatically. "Apparently me paying for him to join me on a two-week cruise with all the sun, surf, and sex he could handle was crossing a line."

I barked out a laugh. Okay, so maybe his game face was better than mine. "Sounds like Pretty Woman. Was he a hooker too?"

He snorted. "No, just a guy who..."

"You had a gentleman's agreement with?"

"Sure. Let's go with that."

I chuckled, and he smiled. I wasn't sure what to do with

him for almost two weeks, but then I had an idea. "Because it's just us, want me to show you how to sail?"

His eyes shot to mine, wide and full of spark. "Serious?"

"Why not." I shrugged. "But don't worry, I'm not going to put you to work or anything. Just the basics. I can't fill in your time like your friend might have, but I can try."

CHAPTER THREE

STUART

HOW THE CONVERSATION between us flirted around sex, I'll never know. Foster was sexy as hell—the sun had kissed his skin, bleached the tips of his hair. Tanned, sand-coloured hair and eyes as blue as the sky above us. He had a deep voice, a warm laugh, and hands that looked strong. He was barefoot, wore tan cargo shorts and a blue shirt with a Tropic Heat logo. He looked as sleek and polished as his luxury yacht yet as free and wild as the coast he worked on.

It was an interesting combination. Like I said, a sexy-as-hell combination.

I'd wondered how these twelve days would go, just me and the skipper, and I worried it could be awkward. But from what I could tell, given it had only been a few hours, I thought we might get along just fine.

I hadn't realised I might ever want to learn a single thing about sailing until he mentioned it. But it was like a challenge, and if there was anything guaranteed to interest me, it was learning new and challenging things. He showed me the boom, the mainsail, the headsail or jib, the sail cover, the lines, and the rigging. "Lines? Aren't they just ropes?"

He laughed. "Nope. Nautical terms are different. Do you want the technical reason it's not called a rope, or do you not really care?"

"Technical term."

He cocked his head a little. I think he liked my direct answer. "Ropes are what lines are made of, and a coiled rope is unassigned a specific job. It's just rope. But lines have a specific purpose. Anchor line or dock line. And the line assigned to pull up the mainsail, or the main as we call it, is called the halyard."

"Nautical terms are confusing. Like port side and stern. I mean, who made that shit up?"

He laughed. "I guess that's what happened in the Middle Ages when sailors all around the world needed a common language."

I almost snorted. "True. I guess I didn't think of it like that."

He stepped around the yacht like he was on dry land, familiar with every inch of it. And where I was a little unsteady and uncertain, he moved with it, fluid and gentle, like he was an extension of the yacht, of the ocean.

He showed me the GPS, how the dual steering wheels worked, how to kick over the engine, how to drop anchor. "Everything's electric on this yacht," he explained. "For the price of her, so it should be." He smiled when he said that.

"I'd hate to think what this yacht cost," I mused.

"Well, it's my house and office," he added, running his hand along the white edge of the cabin housing. I mean, coach housing. Ugh, God. I'd never learn the terminology.

"Your house?"

"Sure. I live on board."

I stared at him. "This is everything you own? No house, no other belongings?"

My blunt questions didn't offend him. He just smiled wider. "This is everything I need. Believe me, I've had the apartments, cars, expensive suits, every hi-tech gadget available. I was happy to leave it behind."

I turned his words over in my head. *I was happy to leave it behind.* God, if only. "Wow."

He stared at me for a long while before giving me a sympathetic smile. "How about that swim?"

I let out a slow breath. "Sounds really good."

"Reckon you can hoist the main?"

"On my own? Have you lost your mind?"

He laughed at my expression. "Come on, I'll do it. You watch for next time."

He managed it with as much effort as breathing, talking as he did it. "When I was a kid, I'd have to work the lines and sails manually. Now I just press a button for most of them. I can manage the sails from the cockpit. A necessity considering I'm doing it all single-handed."

I watched everything he did. "Did you always sail? Even as a kid?"

"My dad sailed out of Rushcutters."

"Sydney?"

He nodded. "Born and bred."

"How long have you been doing this for?"

"Six years." He flashed me a winning smile as he tightened the rope... line... halyard. Whatever. And soon enough, the sail was billowing in the breeze, and we began to move. "You ready for this?" he asked, moving quickly, adeptly, back to the seat that spanned the width of the boat, and took one of the steering wheels.

I clambered to join him with what felt like all the grace of an elephant to his gazelle. "Here, take the wheel," he said.

"Shit." I did as he asked. The wheel itself was huge and sleek wrapped with fine leather so it wouldn't get slippery.

"Relax. It's just like driving a car. Kind of." Then he shot me a look. "You can drive a car, right?"

I laughed at that. "Yeah, of course."

And he was right. Once I relaxed a little, I began to actually enjoy it. The wind, the cruising speed. He helped me steer it a little—because it wasn't like driving a car at all—and soon enough, we rounded a headland and found the small private beach he mentioned earlier. "Oh, wow," I murmured.

It was stunning. Absolutely stunning. The whitest sand, blue-green water, palm trees, and a tropical forest.

He brushed past me, hoisted himself up onto the deck to check something, then came back to the cockpit and had the mainsail in in no time at all. He made everything look so easy. Then he was back and tapped me on the knee. "Scoot over."

I slid into the corner and he sat beside me, steering the boat as we drifted into the inlet seamlessly. When he'd found a spot he deemed perfect, he let me drop anchor. Which was pressing a button, but still. I got to drop anchor.

I was grinning like a kid in a lolly shop, and he chuckled when he looked at me. "It's pretty cool, yeah?"

"It's amazing." I took in the scenery, 360 degrees of tropical perfection. "I need better words than wow and amazing."

He laughed. "You packed your swimming gear?"

"Oh, of course."

I went down to my room and changed into my swimmers and remembered I'd only packed a pair of white Speedos. I'd thought I'd be sunbathing with Jason, and he'd always appreciated my arse in the bare minimum. I now regretted not packing board shorts. I pulled out all I'd packed and had nothing but cargos and golf shorts. I couldn't very well wear them swimming.

Fuck.

With an almighty sigh, I changed into the Speedos, adjusted my dick, grabbed a towel, wrapped it around my waist, and went back up into the cockpit. Foster was adjusting something at the back of the boat.

"You good?" he asked, which I took to be his way of asking if all was well.

"Yeah. All good."

He afforded me a smile, then went straight back to business. "Okay, there's some things I need to show you. It's important."

His tone was serious, so I guessed it was a safety issue. And I was right. "You have to make sure the ladder is down before you dive in. I can't stress this enough."

"I've seen that movie," I admitted, "where they all jumped in and the ladder wasn't down. They couldn't get back in and drowned."

He nodded. "True story. Normally there's more than just two people, and I stay aboard while they swim then dive in real quick after they're all back safely."

Again, he mentioned that it was just us two. "Yeah, sorry. He didn't give me any notice."

"No, that's fine. It's no bother to me. We just need to adjust, that's all." He looked at the sky and the ocean around us. "Conditions are perfect. We have no worries. I just have to give you the rundown, by law."

"Yeah, fair enough. I appreciate it."

He smiled, finally. "Now, sunscreen?"

"Oh." It was pretty obvious I hadn't thought of that. "I packed some. Just haven't put it on yet."

"I have some." He cleared his throat and made a face. "Need um... need me to help with that?" He lifted the seat in the cockpit and took out a bottle of SPF 50. "Being from Brisbane, you're kind of used to the sun, but I've had some folks from other parts of the world that resembled lobsters after day one."

"I can imagine." I looked at the sunscreen he was holding and held in the breath I wanted to sigh out. "If you could do my back, that'd be great." I turned and heard the pop of the lid, and then his strong, warm hands were on my shoulders. The cream was cool but he rubbed it in, squeezing my shoulders a bit.

"You're tight as hell."

I snorted. "You're not the first man to tell me that."

His hands stilled, and his voice was lower. "Oh. I meant in the shoulders."

I shot a grin over my shoulder at him. "Yeah, I knew that. I just couldn't leave that punchline hanging."

He finished rubbing in the sunscreen, using sure hands and strong strokes. I had to admit, I liked his touch.

"You work out," he said. It was a statement, not a question. Was his voice husky? Or was it my imagination?

"Yeah. Helps with stress."

He squeezed my shoulders again. "Doesn't seem to be working too well."

I let my head fall back as he dug his thumbs in. "Yeah. It's a work in progress. And anyway, that's what I'm here for. To relax and de-stress."

"Then you've come to the right place," he said, pulling his hands away.

I turned to face him, thankful the towel was knotted at my front, giving me a little room to hide any appreciation that might be showing in my Speedos. "Need me to return the favour?"

He turned quickly and pulled his shirt off. "Sure."

His shoulders were broad, his arms were well-muscled, his waist was trim. I smeared sunscreen all over his back and went to work. "You're not tight at all."

Now it was he who snorted. "Can't say I've ever been told that."

I laughed at that. "I should hope not."

He rolled his shoulders. "I haven't had one stressful day in six years."

Then I ran my fingers down his collarbones and over his biceps, rubbing some sunscreen there. Not really needing to touch him there, but I had a good excuse. He was firm under my hands, his skin tanned and beautiful, and I longed to see the front. "Lucky you. Sounds like this was the best thing you ever did."

"It really was." He turned to face me, and I wasn't disappointed in his chest. Oh no... not disappointed at all. Tanned, with the perfect amount of chest hair, darker than his dirty blond. He didn't exactly have a six pack, but he was most definitely well-defined all over.

That thought made me shiver.

Thankfully, he didn't notice. He was too busy squirting sunscreen on his hand, and then he handed it to me before he proceeded to rub it over his chest and stomach, his arms, then finally his face. And I was still stuck staring at him. He was gorgeous.

Shit.

Why did I have to be wearing tiny, white Speedos?

Needing the distraction, I busied myself lathering on sunscreen, and when I was done, I couldn't put it off any longer. I walked to the back of the yacht, dropped my towel, and dived into the crystal-clear, aqua-coloured water.

I wondered if he watched me drop the towel. Part of me hoped he had.

It was probably ridiculous. And utterly futile. Even if he was interested in guys, he'd probably have some company policy about fraternising with paying clients. Much like I did; never get involved personally with clients. It was a good work ethic to have, and if I lived by it, I certainly couldn't blame Foster for doing the same.

But damn, he was hot. And it was just the two of us...

Jesus, Stuart. Get a grip.

I broke the surface and let the salt air fill my lungs. The water was glorious and a welcome relief to the heat and humidity of the tropical summer. I could see the white sand at the bottom, just a few metres down. We were close enough to shore that I could swim to the beach. It was maybe fifty metres. I did ten times that to finish my gym sessions... And then I thought that was a great idea. So I set off at a leisurely pace, nice long strokes, and kept my breathing even until I could stand up.

I stayed waist deep and turned to face the yacht. And wow, didn't it look glorious against the backdrop. It sure was a beautiful boat. Foster stood on the back and waved, and I could see the smile on his face from where I stood. I waved back, then proceeded to float on my back for a moment or two. There were no waves. The inlet was protected, and I could float easily.

It felt amazing.

Being immersed in cool water, the warm sun on my front, the silence, the feeling of being removed. There was no stress here. No crazy deadlines, no boss yelling, no customers complaining, or worse, crying. No co-workers trying to talk themselves down in the bathrooms, no assistants looking nervously around the offices.

Nothing but the sound of my own heartbeat in my ears and the sound of the water lapping at my skin.

This was just what the doctor ordered.

I stood again and walked up the beach. It was completely private, not another soul for miles, with the exception of Foster, but even he was giving me space. I walked up onto the whitest sand I'd ever seen, silken and hot under the sun, and I put my hand on one of the many palm trees. It was rough and warm, and the wood felt amazing.

I'd always loved the texture of different objects, obscure things, and this was perfect. Everything felt amazing. It felt different here. Like a vacation should.

Sure, I was disappointed Jason had opted out, but I couldn't change that now, and at any rate, I liked Foster. And I was certain he wouldn't be sharing stories with me or teaching me the basics of sailing if Jason were here. He wouldn't have offered to rub sunscreen on my back, that was for sure.

Surely a little holiday flirting was allowed. It didn't have to lead anywhere, but a sexy smile and laugh and actual conversation were sometimes just as therapeutic as sex. Especially sex that didn't mean anything.

I wasn't tired of one-night hook-ups. Was I?

Not that it really mattered. I didn't have a choice. My work was such a commitment, I didn't have time for anyone. It wouldn't be fair to them. No, my career was number one, and casual hook-ups were all I'd ever need.

I walked along the beach a bit, wondering if rubbing in sunscreen was all Foster was interested in. His hands had felt so good on me, I certainly wouldn't mind his touch on other parts of my body. Would it make things awkward between us if I asked? What if he said no?

What if he said yes?

Jesus. He could be happily married for all I knew.

I looked back to the yacht. Foster wasn't on the deck or the cockpit or in the water, so I assumed he was in the cabin. I didn't mind; I felt a million miles away from everything, yet somehow sure Foster knew my whereabouts at every second. So I kept walking at a slow pace, and by the time I'd made my way back down the beach, Foster was sitting on the back of his yacht, his feet in the water. He was now wearing board shorts, and he gave me a wave and I could see his smile.

I reckoned I'd left him alone enough or worried him enough about what the hell I was doing, so I waded back out and began a slow, languid swim back to the yacht. I pulled up a few metres from him and trod water, taking in his sexy, shirtless form. "Getting in?" I asked him.

"Maybe."

"It's divine."

He gave me a pouty smile and kicked his feet in the water, but he leaned back on his hands and stared at me as if he was trying to decide. It was a curious gaze, then he bit on his bottom lip as though he was weighing up whether to cross a line or not.

Oh yeah. I recognised conflict of interest when I saw it.

Maybe he was reading my mixed signals. Maybe he was giving them. Maybe he bedded every client who boarded his yacht; maybe he was wondering how to offer his special services to me.

Maybe I should make it a whole lot easier on him. Maybe I should lay my cards on the table, make him do the same, and see which one of us held the ace.

I swam up to the yacht, took the ladder in both hands, and hauled myself out of the water, slow step by slow step. He watched every movement and let out a slow breath when I sat right next to him. So maybe the white Speedos weren't such a bad idea after all because he drank in every part of me.

I might have made a little show by patting my towel over my body, which he tried not to watch but failed, and I smiled when he licked his bottom lip.

"You should totally dive right in," I said, meaning every ounce of double entendre I could load into just six words. "It's worth it."

He cleared his throat and looked back out to the beach before running a hand through his hair. "You're probably right," he replied, getting to his feet and diving in before I could say another word.

I was pretty good at reading people. It was what made me brilliant at my job. And I was sure I was reading him right. Yeah, the white Speedos hadn't been a mistake after all.

CHAPTER FOUR

FOSTER

WHITE SPEEDOS. Tiny white Speedos at that. Why did he have to wear them, of all things? I don't care how many linings they had, those tight white swimmers barely concealed anything. And as if they weren't revealing enough when dry, but wet? I could see everything. Every line, every vein, every single thing.

He was uncut, almost hairless. His balls were drawn up tight, his cock snug across to the left.

How was I supposed to get through two weeks of this? I'd barely made it one day.

White Speedos were my favourite. Tiny white Speedos made my mouth water and my dick take notice. Like it hadn't noticed already.

I liked the way he listened when I taught him about the yacht, the way he asked questions, the way a line of concentration formed between his eyebrows, how he chewed on his bottom lip. I liked how he used his hands; he liked to touch everything. The smooth fibreglass of the cabin, the feel of the wooden slats on the cockpit, the cords of twined cable and rope in the lines. He liked to touch, that was pretty clear. To feel, to reconcile the texture with the word, the object.

He was tactile.

I liked that a lot.

He took care of his body. He was here to take care of his mind. And I had to remind myself he was a client. The last thing I needed was a lawsuit for sexual harassment if I made a pass and he rejected me.

Despite the look in his eyes.

Despite his play on words.

Despite the blatant display of his body.

Despite his fucking white Speedos.

His tiny white Speedos.

Jesus.

I needed to dive into the water to clear my head and hoped the cool water cleared my libido. This wasn't going to end well. How the hell was I supposed to survive the next two weeks with him, just the two of us? There was nowhere to escape, except for diving into the ocean to put some distance between us. I hadn't expected the intimacy of there being just the two of us. There was no one else to buffer conversation, to absorb our attention. I would have to switch on the TV and pretend I needed to tend to things below deck. Hell, if my dick didn't settle down, I'd have to lock myself in my room.

I stayed close to the yacht and pretended I was doing some hull check while I had the chance, and by the time I hauled my arse back on board, Stuart was lying on his back on the deck, enjoying the sunshine. At least he had his towel around his waist.

Thank God.

I dried off pretending not to notice him. Then he lifted

one leg, bending it at the knee, and his towel fell open to reveal the white swimwear at his hip.

Tease.

"Refreshing, yes?" he said, his eyes still closed.

Oh yes.

"Very."

"I may never want to leave," he murmured. Then he undid his towel completely, revealing his bulge. He opened his eyes, just to watch me watch him. Then he ever so slowly rolled over, lifted his hips, and readjusted his dick, then lowered himself back down and spread his legs.

Damn.

He sighed, and my gaze shot to his face. He smiled as he closed his eyes. "Would you mind hitting me up with the sunscreen again?" he asked.

Fuck.

As if he could sense my hesitance, even with his eyes closed, he added, "I'd hate to get sunburnt."

I was frozen for a split second, so unlike me. This was a terrible idea, but I couldn't very well admit to why without giving myself away. I squirted the cream onto his shoulders and began to rub it in. He rolled his shoulders and stretched his neck as I did my part. If he was playing it up or if he was really that reactive to touch, I could only guess. But the idea took my mind places it shouldn't go. While I wanted to linger, rub harder—hell, I wanted to straddle his thighs and give him a massage he'd never forget—I remembered my job and ignoring my hardening dick, I finished quickly. "Done." I wiped my hands on my towel. "I'll fix you a snack," I said, quickly taking the steps into the cabin.

I leaned against the kitchen cabinets and took a deep breath. *Forget it, Foster. Just do your freakin' job.*

I refixed the towel around my waist, palming my dick

into submission in the process, then washed my hands thoroughly before plating up some cheese, fruit, and crackers. I figured after his swim and walk on the beach and now relaxing in the sun, he'd have worked up an appetite, so I grabbed him a bottle of beer as well.

I carried them back upstairs to find him still lying on his belly, his head turned, his eyes closed. I allowed myself a second to take in his form. Tanned, fit, and white Speedos.

Those fucking white Speedos.

He opened his eyes, and a knowing smirk pulled at his lips.

Fuck.

"Afternoon tea is served," I said like I hadn't just been caught checking him out.

He rolled onto his side, groaning as he sat up. "Oh, swimming and sunshine are like a sedative." He climbed down to sit on the long bench seat. He held his towel, and making no attempt to cover himself, he lay it across his thigh. His dick was half-hard and filled his Speedos deliciously.

God, I was in trouble. He hadn't even been on board a day.

He seemed to like being on display for me. Teasing me, tempting me. There was a slight curl to his lips, daring in his eyes. He ate some cheese, then a strawberry and some honeydew melon, groaning. "This is so good."

I handed over his beer. "For you."

He took it. "Don't you want one too?"

"I don't drink when I have clients on board."

"Oh, right. I keep forgetting this is your actual job, not just a dream holiday."

I chuckled. "Sometimes I forget too." There was more truth to that than I cared to admit. Like ten minutes ago when I was imagining straddling him. A client. Yes, sometimes I forgot this was my actual job. Better to head back to safer waters, so I redirected the conversation. "It's easy to forget when your office looks like this," I said, gesturing to the entire horizon.

"Ever had anyone want to defect?" he asked, sucking on a strawberry. "Run away from their lives and do what you do?"

I ignored the strawberry juice that pooled on his lips and fixed some cheese onto a cracker. I shrugged. "They all talk about it, but no one ever does. It's just a dream for them."

He sighed. "Well, it does seem surreal. You have to admit."

"What? Having enough of the rat race, spending your entire life savings on a yacht, and sailing off into the sunset?" I laughed. "Surreal, yes. Not impossible though."

He took a pull of his beer and looked out at the water. "Some days, I could so easily walk away."

"Then why don't you?"

His gaze shot to mine. "I don't know. Fear of the unknown. Fear of being forgotten, replaced. Lack of financial security." A sad smile tugged at his lips. "It's not that easy."

I held his intense stare. "It's exactly that easy."

"You just walked away?"

I nodded. "Yep. There I was, busting myself, literally killing myself for a boss that, if I had actually dropped dead, would've replaced me by eight the next morning. And it struck me like lightning." I laughed at the memory. "I was in the middle of a meeting. Huge contract, multimillion-dollar businesses, international clients, the deal of a career, and I realised I was just a cog in the machine. I was replaceable, interchangeable, expendable in every way. I'd sacrificed everything for people who didn't give a shit, and it struck me right in the middle of the meeting."

Stuart was watching me, intrigued. "What did you do?"

"I stood up and walked out."

"Just like that?"

I grinned at him. "Just like that."

He let out a breath, then took a drink of his beer. "I couldn't do that. I'm pretty sure my boss would track me down. He seems to think he owns my soul."

I snorted. "They all do. Hell, I was the same. I used to chew people up and spit them out. And for what? To make them miserable? To break them?" I sighed and shook my head sadly. "I often wonder what happened to them."

Stuart studied me for a second, then handed me his beer. I was going to say no but thought, fuck it. I grabbed it, took a long pull, and handed it back to him. "Thanks."

He smiled. "You sound like me. It's what I do for a living. Chewing people up and spitting them out. I'm good at it too. It's why my boss owns me. Well, that, and because when I threatened to leave, he offered me a shitload of money to stay. So maybe he did buy my soul. Some days I think he did."

"What's your field?" I asked.

"Investment banking," he admitted. "Global and capital markets."

Well, I'll be damned. "Mergers and acquisitions, corporate banking, treasury, debt and equity..."

His gaze shot to mine. "You know about that?"

I gave him half a smile. "I know all there is to know about investment banking."

He stared at me. "Is that... is that what you walked away from?"

I nodded. "Yep. Senior analyst for EconAsia."

"Econ...," he mumbled, his eyes wide in disbelief. "The world's largest corporate bank. The financial bridge between China and..." His words trailed away and he stared at me.

"The rest of the world?" I finished for him. "Yep. *That* EconAsia."

He continued to stare at me for a while, with utter disbelief. "You... senior analyst..."

I laughed at his reaction. "Senior analyst for EconAsia, yes. I bought and sold insurance companies, banks and financial institutions all over the world. Hell, I influenced the trade market and economy of small countries, deciding which companies to buy and which to crush, which families kept their homes, which didn't. You wanna talk about selling your soul."

Something flashed in his eyes. Recognition, maybe. Sadness. Understanding. He whispered, "And you walked away."

I held his gaze and gave a nod. "Best thing I ever did."

Stuart swallowed hard and sat back, pulling his towel over his crotch. He looked out over the ocean, the beer in his hand forgotten. I'd obviously thrown him for a six. Or given him something to think about, at least. "I'll just go start fixing dinner," I said and left him to his thoughts.

We'd not long had a snack, but I needed some distance and I figured he did too. I made us a salad and boiled some baby potatoes and was seasoning the steak when Stuart came back down. He put his empty beer bottle in the bin and leaned against the sink next to me. "Anything I can do?"

I got him a fresh beer and he took it with an appreciative smile. "You can sit and relax. We can have dinner any time you like. I thought we might stay here in the inlet tonight. It's a safe spot, and we've already anchored. Unless you want to head further out?"

He sat on the in-built sofa and stretched out his legs. He looked a little sun-kissed and even more relaxed than he had just a few hours ago. "I will leave it in your very capable hands."

"You can have a swim before breakfast if you like. Then we can sail east to Sudbury reef."

"Sounds good."

"I don't know which are more spectacular here; sunrises or sunsets. You'll have to see both and tell me which you prefer."

"Can we eat dinner in the cockpit?" He looked kind of hopeful.

Normally I preferred to eat actual meals at the table in the cabin. Snacks were okay up top, but it was just the two of us. "Sure."

He watched me for a while. "Don't need me to help?"

I gave him a grin. "Nope. The key to being skipper and chef is keeping meals simple. Simple beet and rocket salad, boiled baby potatoes, and steak. It takes all of ten minutes."

"You have it down to an art."

I poked a potato to see if it was cooked. "The real key is knowing what to cook with the conditions outside. If it's rough and stormy, I wouldn't be boiling potatoes."

"What's the worst conditions you've ever encountered?"

"When the cyclone hit three years ago, I had enough warning to head south. I haven't had much worse than a Category 2 storm."

He shuddered. "Was it bad?"

"Not really. I didn't have anyone on board though,

which was a blessing," I explained. "If we get a severe weather warning, the head office will cancel. That doesn't happen often though. Never in my time, anyway. And at any rate, this is Queensland. How does the slogan go? Queensland, beautiful one day..."

"Perfect the next," he finished with a smile. "Unless there's cyclones or Category 5 storms."

I waved him off. "Pfft. Well, you can expect perfect weather for your trip. We might get rain next week, but when are forecasters ever right?" I switched the potatoes off and drained them in the sink. "Anyway, if we can time it right and if the forecast stays true, we should be at Low Island, so if you're worried about seasickness, you have the option of staying on land."

"I'm good with seasickness," he added with a smile. "Otherwise I wouldn't have picked a yacht hire as my only vacation in five years."

I let my head fall back and I groaned. "I don't miss those days. You can have them."

He smiled at that but didn't reply. He watched me put the steaks on the grill plate. "How do you like your steak?"

"Medium, thanks."

Okay, again with the closeness of it just being us two. It was far more intimate than I was used to. I needed a distraction. I nodded toward the small flat-screen TV bracketed to the wall. "You can turn on the TV if you want. Catch some news? Cricket results?"

He looked at the black screen like he was considering it. "You know what? I'd rather not. If the world's gone to hell in the last twelve hours, I don't want to know." He sighed and almost smiled. "Can you do me a favour?"

I shrugged a shoulder. "Sure. As long as it's legal."

He snorted. "If my boss contacts you, tell him there's no

internet connection, no phone connection, and no TV. I may have told him I was uncontactable."

I chuckled. "Deal. Would he have called you even when you're on holiday?"

He raised an eyebrow. "Do you need to even ask?"

I conceded with an eye roll. "Yeah, sorry."

"I haven't turned my phone on since Jason called last night to cancel on me." His lips twisted in an amused pout. "I thought I'd have internet withdrawals or wouldn't know what to do with my hands, but as it turns out, Jason standing me up took care of that dilemma. Well, knowing what to do with my hands, anyway."

I barked out a laugh at his implication. "I don't miss having my phone plastered to my ear twenty hours a day, that's for damn sure. Phone calls, emails, it just never ended. Especially being on a global platform, no one cared what time zone I was in."

"I could imagine."

"You're based in Brisbane, right?" I asked.

He nodded. "Paulington."

Hmm. Paulington was a reputable company, gaining some clout last I'd heard. "You must be good."

"They're trying to move me to Sydney," he said, looking at his beer like he'd forgotten he was holding it.

I turned the steaks. "But?"

"But I'm not interested. I turned down Singapore too." He sighed, long and loud. "But I guess I can't put it off forever. If I want to further my career, that is."

"Do you? Want to further your career?"

He took a long while to answer, frowning. "I don't know. I feel like I'm at a crossroads. Like I need to decide. Do I want the career and wealth, penthouse apartment, sports car, the endless lines of meaningless men? Or do I want a life that isn't those things."

Endless lines of meaningless men. "Sounds familiar."

"And you don't regret your decision?" His eyes were earnest, and I knew this wasn't just a conversational question. This was him asking me for professional and personal advice.

"Not one bit," I answered. "But it was the right decision for me."

He nodded slowly. "Yeah, I know. I need to make the decision for me."

"Can I be honest?"

He nodded.

"It sounds like you've already made up your mind."

"How so?"

"You're questioning your being there. You're questioning whether you want any part of it or not, and that's kind of an answer in itself."

He sighed and leaned his head back against the wall, stretching his legs out, and that look of exhaustion crept over him again. "I was stretched too thin for too long. But I put in for annual holiday leave rather than stress leave. Because... well, you know why."

"Because the sharks circle, non-stop. One whiff of blood in the water and you're gone."

His eyes cut to mine, sharp and knowing. "Non-stop."

I took the steaks off the grill plate and turned the stove top off. I let the meat rest for a bit and plated up the salad and potatoes. "When I left, I had two different prescriptions for blood pressure and stomach ulcers, took headache pills constantly. It's how I dealt with the pressure. Most of the other guys I worked with took cocaine, so I consider myself lucky my vices weren't so bad."

"Well, you were in a different league than me," he mumbled quietly. Then he snorted, smiled, and shook his head. "Where I'm from, I'm the best there is. I'm the king of corporate finance. Compared to you," he said, his smile wry, "I feel like I'm sitting at the kids' table."

I stopped slicing the steak. "Compared to me? I walked away from it. Now I'm a nobody in your world."

He looked up at the ceiling and gave a slight shake of his head. It was pretty clear he didn't agree. "You were swimming in the big league. I'm barely surviving paddling in the kiddies' pool."

"That's bullshit."

He shot me a look. My words obviously surprised him. I finished slicing the steaks and gave him a smile. "It's a different game these days. What's it been? Six years since I left. How long have you been doing it?"

"Six years."

"The world I left behind would be unrecognisable to you. It's so different now; the world gets smaller every day, yet expectations are so much higher. Technology and the internet are wonderful things, and sure, the opportunities are bigger, but bloody hell, so are the demands. How you operate today would run rings around me."

He stared at me and a faint smile tugged at the corner of his mouth. "Maybe."

I added his sliced steak to his salad, added some dressing, and put our plates on a tray. I added another bottle of beer for him, some cutlery, and serviettes. "Dinner is served. Now let's go and see what kind of sunset we're gonna get today."

I carried the tray upstairs and slid it onto the long seat. He sat on one side of it; I sat on the other. I picked up my plate and a fork, and he chuckled. "Ah, I wondered why you sliced the steak up," he said. "Plate in one hand, fork in the other. You've done this before."

I laughed. "Once or twice."

He smiled, then took a forkful of steak and salad. His groan was obscene. "Holy shit," he mumbled around his food. "What is this?"

I grinned at his reaction. "The salad? Roasted beets and pumpkin with rocket. The dressing is my dad's Spanish onion recipe that I'm sworn by blood to keep secret."

He swallowed and licked his lips. "It's amazing." He looked out over the small beach, then back out over the ocean, and shook his head. "Everything here is amazing."

We ate in silence after that, and he drank his beer as we watched the sun set over the horizon. The sky was brilliant shades of pink and orange, the water crystal blue, the quiet between us was pleasant, and I felt oddly serene. I also had the feeling that if we'd met under different circumstances, in a bar or at work, Stuart and I could be friends. I liked him. His gorgeous looks, killer smile, and heart-stopping eyes aside, he was a nice guy.

"You know what?" I said, not really knowing what came over me. "I'm kinda glad your friend Jason didn't come along. I get the feeling you're being the real you because you're not keeping up with who he'd probably expect you to be. You can just be the real you, no pressure, no expectations."

He stared at me for the longest time, searching my eyes. He swallowed hard. "I think you might be right."

CHAPTER FIVE

STUART

FOSTER WAS RIGHT about a lot of things. The sunset was stunning; there was no other way to describe it. And I think he was right about Jason not being on board. If he had been here, I'd still be in professional mode. Jason only knew the professional me, the no-nonsense me that had time constraints and deadlines. Our time together was based purely on sex, and I pretty much had our time together written in my schedule. I could literally slot him in from nine till ten on a Wednesday and Saturday night. He'd turn up, take care of me in all the ways I needed, and be gone.

And now that Foster had pointed that out, that I was now free to be truly me, I had to wonder what the hell I was thinking asking Jason to come in the first place.

Sure, the guaranteed sex would have been nice, but I could see now that soul-soothing relaxation, finding myself —being myself—was more important.

I couldn't remember the last time I'd just got to be me.

That I just got to breathe.

Before the sun had set completely, Foster tidied up and

collected the tray, but I stopped him. "Here, let me take that."

He gawped at me. "I will not."

"Why not?"

"You're my guest. My client, paying me to look after you."

I rolled my eyes. "It's just us two. I can't sit down while you clean up after me."

"Why not? That's exactly what you should do."

"Have you ever had a mutiny?"

His eyes went wide. "A mutiny?"

"Yeah, isn't that what it's called when the crew argue with the captain?"

"A mutiny is more of a takeover."

I took the tray from him. "Then I'm taking over. I'll wash, you dry."

I grinned at his expression and went down the stairs to the galley. He was right behind me. "Stuart. You really don't have to do that."

"I want to, and you wouldn't deny a paying client what he wanted to do, would you?"

He sagged. "You're used to getting what you want, aren't you?"

"Always. I don't take no for an answer." I found the detergent and filled the sink with hot water, then collected the dirty pan and utensils. "You're a very tidy cook."

He gave me a disgruntled huff, but then he almost smiled. "When you're the cook and the cleaner, you soon learn that minimalism is good. And there's a dishwasher."

"This won't take us long," I replied. And in no time at all, I had everything washed and Foster had everything dried. "See? Many hands make light work. Or something like that, my mum says."

He folded the tea towel and hung it neatly to dry. "Well, thank you for your help."

I opened the small fridge and pulled out two beers, cracked the lid on one, and handed it to him. "Go on, I promise not to tell anyone." He looked like he might argue, so I added, "It's a mutiny, remember?"

He snarled at me but took the beer. "You haven't even been on board a day and I've broken three of my rules already."

"Three?"

"Letting you clean up, one. Drinking beer, that's two. And the third, I left you alone on deck when I got in the water."

I popped the lid on my beer and took a swig to hide my smile. I sat at the table, and looking at him, I nodded. "Ah, the white Speedos. Did you dive in the water to hide from me or to cool down? I mean, I know those Speedos are hot."

He blushed. "I didn't..."

"You totally did."

He plonked himself at the table across from me, our feet almost touching. He sighed and took a long pull of his beer. "I wasn't expecting them. That's all I'm admitting to."

I laughed. "I'm kidding, really. I was nervous about wearing them. I should've packed some board shorts, but I'd packed when I thought Jason was coming and forgot to take them out when he'd cancelled."

He took another drink of his beer and stared at the bottle when he spoke. "Well, I can't say I'm sorry."

I grinned. "You like?"

He rolled his eyes. "You know you look good in them."

Now I laughed. "What can I say? They emphasise my best feature."

His cheeks tinted pink, and he cleared his throat. He was still staring at his bottle. "And what would that be?"

I laughed again. "My arse, of course. Why? See something else you like?"

I was only joking when I'd said it, but wow, something flashed in Foster's eyes when he shot a glance at me. "I uh... I have certain rules."

"Which you're quite happy to break, apparently," I said, nodding to the beer bottle he was fascinated with.

He drained the rest of his bottle, then stared right at me, and the warm night just got a whole lot hotter. The space between us felt both far too close and far too wide, and it crackled with tension. He licked the corner of his mouth, his pink tongue sending a jolt of want straight to my dick. But then he looked away, breaking the trance we both seemed to be under. "I better go and do a final check up on deck," he said, his voice rough and strained. "Then I'll be turning in for the night. Thank you for helping me clean up after dinner. Sleep well." He left the bottle on the galley bench and darted up the stairs, disappearing into the night.

So there it was; my cards were now officially on the table. And I knew desire when I saw it. The way his eyes darkened and sharpened, the way his cheeks flushed, and the way his breath hitched ever so slightly.

I was adept at reading people. It's what made me good at my job. I knew how to read their reactions, and I knew when to apply pressure and when to retreat.

He might be physically attracted to me, but his moral compass was driving this ship. In more ways than one. He'd put as much distance between us as this boat allowed, so I would give him the distance he sought.

If he changed his mind, he knew where to find me. It wasn't like we could exactly hide from each other on a fourteen-metre yacht in the middle of the ocean. So yes, I'd let him decide. I could push a little harder to see if the spark of desire in his eyes would catch fire. I mean, we were barely on day one of twelve, and we'd already blurred some of his rules. I couldn't wait to see what day two brought.

With that in mind, I put our empty bottles in the bin and went to bed.

I NEVER KNEW I could sleep so well. I had fully intended to listen for Foster to come back down into the cabin, the sound of a door closing or toilet flushing, but I heard nothing. I'd also fully intended to take care of my semi-hard dick when I crawled into bed, but as soon as my head hit the pillow, the lull of the water and the gentle rock of the boat had me out like a light.

I woke with no clue what the time was, only that it was still dark outside my little window. But I heard footsteps in the quiet and I knew Foster was up. By the time I'd taken a piss, washed my face, and brushed my teeth, I found him up in the cockpit looking at one of the screens he'd shown me yesterday. The sky was beginning to lighten, enough so I could see him, the water, and the coastline. It looked fresh and peaceful, remarkably beautiful, Foster included.

"Morning," I said as I joined him. I wasn't going to pretend my implied offer last night didn't happen, but I wasn't going to make it awkward either. I was going to flirt and be playful, and I sure as hell wasn't getting out of my white Speedos any time soon. I had a towel around my waist, my chest bare.

"Morning," he replied, giving me a quick smile before turning back to the screen. "Sleep okay?"

"Like the dead. I don't know if it's the water or the boat or the silence, but I haven't slept that well in... well, years."

"Good. I'm glad to hear that." He smiled. "I'm just checking the tides and wind direction."

"How's it looking?"

"Perfect. We should be good to sail northeast after breakfast. How does that sound?"

"Sounds great. Am I still right to have a swim before-hand?" I asked, looking toward the back of the yacht.

"Sure. Water's a beautiful twenty-six degrees." He turned and looked at me directly. "Breakfast'll be ready when you're done."

I held his gaze and pulled at my towel, revealing the swimsuit he liked so much, barely confining my semi-morning wood. His gaze went straight to my dick, then to my face, and he stared at me with a *you bastard* expression as he fought a smile. "Excellent," I said, grinning right back at him. I was going to ask him to join me but figured the eyeful I just gave him was invitation enough.

I dropped the towel, bent over, and lowered the stairs like he'd shown me—while pointing my arse right at him—and dived cleanly into the water.

It was a fresh way to wake up properly, and I broke the surface with a laugh. I turned to face the yacht and trod water, smiling when Foster came to the back of the boat, probably to see what I was laughing at. "This is amazing," I said. "I should wake up to this every day."

He grinned and replied, "It's not exactly terrible."

"You should get in," I called out.

He stared for a full three seconds. "Maybe later," he said, before going back to whatever he was doing.

Maybe later.

Maybe we'd be doing a lot of things later... I hoped we

would be. He was interested, that was for sure. The way he'd looked at me when I pulled the towel off told me all I needed to know. He looked like he wanted to eat me for days, and I was totally on board with that. Eleven more days, to be exact.

I floated on my back and grinned up at the cloudless sky. It was getting lighter, the sun was almost beginning to break the horizon, and something occurred to me. It hit me like a jolt that had me struggling to get upright, to tread water again.

What if he wasn't single?

What if he had a boyfriend?

A husband? A wife?

Oh God. Maybe he was being polite because I was his private client for two weeks and I was making him incredibly uncomfortable. Maybe he was trying to find a way to let me down without offending me.

Because while Foster might have his rules, I had mine too.

My golden rule: I didn't touch what belonged to other people.

I didn't play second fiddle for anyone. And I didn't sneak around or cheat. I didn't do messy relationships for a start. Or complications.

I didn't have time for that kind of involvement anyway, but there was a certain integrity to be upheld when I invited men into my bed. If they were single and free to do what they wanted, then hell yes, the more the merrier. If they were in a mutually open relationship, hell yes, the more the merrier. If they were a couple who liked to enjoy a third, hell fucking yes.

But if a guy was looking to be unfaithful to his boyfriend or husband, then absolutely not. I'd had guys tell me we should fuck anyway because *my* conscience was clear, but that wasn't the point. Relationships were a big fucking deal; a matter of heart and trust. And if a guy thought nothing of that, then he certainly was never getting a piece of me.

One-night stands, casual fuck-buddies, blowjobs in nightclub bathrooms were all part of any given weekend for me. But in the clubs I went to, in the bars I frequented, I knew who was single, and I knew with just one look who was lying.

I swam back to the ladder and climbed up, drying off before wrapping the towel around me and tying it off at my waist, just as Foster was coming back up out of the cabin with a tray.

"Back already?" he asked, sliding it onto the seat. "Let me just grab the coffee."

I sat down, water dripping from my hair, running down my neck. It felt nice against the breeze. It was just after six o'clock in the morning and it was already warm. I let the towel fall open a bit, not being crude, but revealing enough that he'd notice.

Foster reappeared with a plunger of coffee and two cups. I took one and he poured me a cup before filling his and sitting on the other side of the tray. And yes, he noticed how my towel was open just so. He licked his lips and looked at my face. "How was the water?"

"Perfect."

He met my eyes then, his cheeks tinting pink, knowing he'd been caught. Then he shook his head a little, as if to clear it, and nodded at the tray. "Yoghurt, granola, fruit. Help yourself. I get the organic granola that's made locally."

"Looks healthy," I said. And it did. Beautiful, even. "With a diet like this, it's no wonder you look so good."

He sipped his coffee and blushed some more before putting his cup on the tray and taking a bowl of yoghurt. "It's a pretty physical job. It's not hard to stay in shape. I can make you some eggs on toast if you'd prefer?"

I watched him pile on some granola and berries. "No, this is perfect," I replied. "The swim and the sunrise... It's kind of a spectacular way to start a day. You won't ever get tired of it?"

He snorted. "Never."

I hated to delve into personal-question territory, but I needed to ask this before I went any further with the whole flirt-and-playful routine. "So, this is your house, so to speak. No port you call home? No special someone who expects you to moor your yacht next to his? Or hers?"

He chewed his mouthful thoughtfully, and he smiled as he swallowed. "No port, as such. I have a post office box in Cairns and a registered mooring. If that makes Cairns home, I'm not sure. I guess it does."

He left my other question unanswered. Or maybe that was his way of answering it. I couldn't deny I was a little disappointed; he was gorgeous and clearly very good with his hands, and I was certain that would be the same in bed. But it just wasn't meant to be. I put my coffee down and fixed my towel, covering myself completely. "Yeah, I guess it does."

He seemed amused by my reaction, and curious. He ate his yoghurt while I served some up for myself, and we watched the sunrise in silence. He kept glancing at me, his smile widening each time, and eventually I raised an eyebrow at him.

"What's so funny?"

He put his empty bowl back on the tray. "Were you trying to ask if there's anyone in my life who would mind me sailing around the tropics alone with a hot single guy who wears tiny white Speedos?"

"Maybe." I licked my spoon and he watched. "I don't touch what belongs to someone else."

His gaze met mine, and he tilted his head just a bit. "Is that right?"

"Yes," I answered without hesitation. A slow smile crept across his lips. "Something funny about that?"

"No, not at all. I just got the impression that you were —" He made a face. "—open to whatever might come your way."

"You thought I was some corporate financial hotshot who'd have anyone he wanted in his bed, whenever he wanted? Fast deals, fast cars, fast sex, not caring about collateral damage."

"I've lived in your world, remember?" he said, his gaze unflinching. "I know how it is. It's fast and full on. You have power in certain circles and men are drawn to that."

I heard what he was saying, and one thing I'd learned in my career was that criticism was quite often harshest when it hit close to home. I'd also learned how to let it roll off me. I put my bowl down and shrugged. "True. Sure, I've had guys offer to suck my dick under my desk if they thought it would get them a sweeter deal. But if you truly know what it's like in my world and what it's like to be the best, then you'd know I do background checks on every person who crosses my path, and I know if they're dating, engaged, married, divorced, straight, bi, gay. If they're anything but single, they're not on my radar." I popped a blueberry in my mouth. "Plus, I don't have anyone from the corporate world in my bed. I like to be fucked into the mattress, and the very last thing I need is to meet an acquaintance in a boardroom, if you know what I mean. They can hold all the power in the bedroom they want, but I would *never* let anyone hold that kind of power over me in my job."

He chewed the inside of his cheek and studied the coastline for a while, a dozen different emotions flickering over his face. Was my comment about being fucked into the mattress too much? Did it make him uncomfortable? Did he like it? He stared out at the ocean, not giving much away. After a while, he said, "I'm not seeing anyone. No one to moor my yacht next to, as you put it, and certainly no one to care if I spend two weeks with a guy wearing tiny white Speedos."

"Hot guy," I amended, trying not to smile.

He shot me an incredulous look. "Pardon?"

"Before, you said 'hot guy wearing tiny white Speedos.' I was correcting you."

He grinned, the eye-crinkling kind, and held my stare. "Silly me. I forgot what kind of arrogance it took to run in M&A."

I smirked at him and hitched the towel up my thighs so the fabric bunched over my dick. "Don't confuse arrogance with honesty."

He looked down at my display of skin, his eyes raking over me like a touch. I pushed the knot of the towel at my waist past my navel, revealing more skin and my happy trail, and gave my dick a palm as I stretched my legs out. The droplets of water on my skin were replaced with sweat. "You were right about one thing though," I said. "The sunrise is as pretty as the sunset, but boy, it sure is *hot* already."

Foster bit back a groan, shot to his feet, and leapt up to the back of the yacht, taking his shirt off as he went. "I'm just gonna cool off," he said before I heard the splash behind me.

I laughed and gave my dick a squeeze. So he was single and interested. It was just his 'no sex with clients' rule that was holding him back, which I was sure he was warring with right then. But I knew I'd win, I always did. He'd give in eventually. It was like catching fish; you had to let out a little line before you could reel them in. So I could act coy, show some skin, be forthright, and be downright slutty. He was a smart man, economically minded, and I could match him in intellectual conversation, stimulating his mind while wearing nothing but my white Speedos, stimulating him elsewhere. Oh yes, playful flirting was my very favourite mating ritual.

I got up on my knees and peered over the back of the yacht. He was just a few metres away, treading water and smiling. "Feel better?" I asked.

He laughed and shook his head but swam back to the ladder and climbed aboard. He was dripping wet, his hair slicked back, his board shorts clinging to his body and bunching in all the right places. Realising he'd forgotten a towel in his haste to cool off, I stood up and undid my towel and threw it to him. He caught it and rubbed it over his hair and face, then he held it to his chest but stopped when he realised I was now standing there wearing nothing but my swimmers. My tiny white swimmers that barely hid my semi-hard dick. All this thinking about reeling him into the bedroom was turning me on. I stood there pleased and proud while he ogled me, letting him know what he could have if he wanted.

He blinked out of his trance and patted his face again with the towel. Oh yes, he'd give in for sure. Smiling, I picked up the breakfast tray. "I'll take care of this," I said. "While you take care of..." I glanced at his crotch. I didn't need to finish my sentence.

I already had the sink full of hot soapy water when he came down into the galley. He seemed to have collected himself and didn't baulk at seeing me still wearing just my Speedos. "Is there something wrong with the dishwasher?" he asked like he was trying very hard not to look below eye level.

"Not at all. But it's two plates, two spoons, two cups. Won't take a second."

He frowned. "You really don't have to do that."

"I don't mind." I ignored him and had the few things washed before he could argue. I grabbed the tea towel and picked one of the bowls, then leaned against the sink as I dried it. "Aren't we sailing northeast soon?"

I wondered how much restraint it took for him to maintain eye contact, given my attire. "Ah, yeah. Did you want to wear some shorts or something...?"

I smirked at him. "Are there any safety rules regarding the wearing of swimwear while sailing?"

"No."

"Then, no. I'm fine wearing this. Are you fine with me wearing this?"

His eyes narrowed, his jaw bulged, and he fought a smile. But he said nothing. So I put the dried bowl down and took the other one, then proceeded to dry it while biting my bottom lip so I didn't grin too hard. "I didn't think you'd have a problem with it."

CHAPTER SIX

FOSTER

THOSE FUCKING WHITE SPEEDOS. And that fucking smirk. And those damn eyes, and that trail of dark hair that disappeared behind the fabric that barely concealed anything. His defined thighs, his abs, his shoulders... Did I mention his smirk?

Get a grip, Foster. You've dealt with guys like him before.

All bravado and ego. Though I was sure something was different with him. He was vulnerable here, trying to de-stress and re-evaluate his life, his career choice. Yet he still had that air of righteousness. What did he tell me? Not to confuse arrogance with honesty?

God, wasn't that the truth.

The problem was, when I looked at him, I saw myself. Ten years ago, I was just like him. And maybe it was arrogance, but it stemmed from being the best. Me saying I was the best in mergers and acquisitions wasn't arrogance; it was the truth.

So Stuart saying that to me struck a familiar chord, a memory of who I used to be. I didn't miss my old life, not one part of it. I prided myself on excellence back then, as I still did today. Only now my office wasn't at the top of a building in Sydney or Singapore. It was a fourteen-metre yacht and my market was the Whitsundays.

No, I didn't miss my old life.

But I did miss the challenge of coming out on top. Seeing who could hold their ground the longest, who had the balls to wait until the other folded under pressure.

And I wondered which of us, me or Stuart, would fold first.

He was playing me, hard. He was putting on a show, playing with words and innuendos, hitching his towel to reveal the silken skin where his thigh met his hip. Giving me the hottest set of "take me to bed and fuck me" eyes I'd ever seen, and his tongue would caress his bottom lip and I wanted to taste it, to suck it into my mouth, and...

Fucking hell.

At this rate, I'd need to dive into the water every twenty minutes. Having to remove myself and throw myself into the ocean, just so I didn't bend him over the control panel and teach him a lesson for teasing me, was bad enough.

God, now I was thinking about doing that.

But I liked how he'd backed off when he thought I was already taken. I liked how he had standards in regards to not bedding just anyone. Jesus, when I'd been in his shoes a decade ago, I hadn't much cared for rules. Willing and condoms were the only two rules I had.

I wasn't wrong when I said men threw themselves at powerful people, and if they'd looked at me twice, there was an exchange of bodily fluids soon after. It wasn't as though I never cared if they wore wedding rings or not, it was that I never thought to notice.

I didn't then, but I would now.

Stuart was a new generation of financier. And although

I didn't miss my old life, I did envy him a little. The power was a pedestal, and guys either wanted to be him or wanted to be with him, and that was a heady thing. But even after only a day, I could tell he had integrity, and that was something that couldn't be bought.

He also had a hot arse and those freakin' Speedos framed it like a work of art.

I was pretty certain it'd be me who folded first.

He was playing me like a violin, and I couldn't even be pissed about it. The rules I'd enforced when I first started this private charter business were getting a little hazy around the edges, and I was just waiting to give in to him.

After he'd tidied up from breakfast—which was my job, not his—he clapped his hands together. "Right then, Captain. Show me how you sail."

"You need a floatation device on before we go anywhere."

"Really?"

"If you intend to be on deck with me, yes."

He shrugged. "Okay."

I got the waist belt floatation device out and held it up. "Here, put this on."

He cocked an eyebrow at me. "Is that a bum-bag or a belt?"

"Were you expecting floaties?" I snorted. "They've come a long way since the old life vests."

He laughed and clipped it on, but it was kind of loose on his trim waist. He bit his bottom lip. "I don't think this one is tight enough," he said, holding the strap and grinning at me.

Of course he had it so the clasp was sitting right above his crotch. I looked him right in the eye and pulled it, hard. His whole body jerked forward with the movement, so we were almost touching. And of course he stared up at me and grinned. "How's that?" I asked.

"So much better," he whispered. His smile became something dirty and flirty.

He was being all cute and shit, which I didn't mind one bit. And truthfully, pulling up anchor and sailing was a much-needed distraction. I gave him orders and he followed them to the letter. He was astute, careful, and never questioned my authority or knowledge. He was the perfect student.

He was also wearing nothing but Speedos and the belt, grinning into the wind. He even put up his hand and let out a 'woo-hoo' as we hit top speed, the look on his face one of complete joy and freedom.

I knew exactly how he felt.

I took us away from the coastline. Though the water under us was deep, it was crystal-clear and azure blue. "You know where you're going, right?" he yelled over the wind.

I laughed, and letting go of the wheel, I waved him over to the GPS which showed our position on the chart. It was more protected in the cockpit near the cabin so I didn't have to yell. "See here?" I pointed to our destination. "At this speed, we'll be there in forty-five minutes."

The wind tousled his hair, and for the first time since I'd met him, he had life in his eyes. "This is incredible!"

"I know." I took him back to the wheel. "Stand here," I instructed. "Keep her steady."

The shine in his eyes deepened and the span of his grin grew wider. He hadn't stopped grinning yet. I pointed out our direction and he nodded, and I couldn't remember the last time I'd had a client enjoy sailing so much. I'd never had anyone want to learn, and I'd certainly never had one-on-one lessons. I'd always loved sailing. Always. But there was something special about experiencing the joy of his first time at the helm.

I let him bring it around the bottom of the reef and I dropped the mainsail, and once it was done, I turned to find him glued to his post, grinning from ear to ear. It did stupid things to my heart, and I told myself I was just caught up in his excitement. And I was; it was true. But the way my belly tightened was something else entirely.

I joined him at the wheel, liking the excuse to stand close to him. We'd slowed down considerably with just the jib, but there was something peaceful about the lazy pace. "We're going to bring her around and follow the reef line. Keep an eye on your depth."

I knew these waters and we had plenty of room under keel, but he didn't know that. His gaze focused, his attention sharp, and he did everything right. I lowered the jib and secured the line and sighed. "This is my favourite part," I said. "This, when the sails come down and we just..." I put my hands out and moved to the beat of the ocean. "There's a peacefulness you won't find anywhere else."

Stuart nodded like he understood completely. "I have never seen any place so beautiful," he said, taking in the sights at every direction. "And the silence? I could get used to this." Then he put his hand on my arm. "Thank you."

He said it with such sincerity, I couldn't doubt it came from his heart. "You're welcome."

"Can I swim here?"

I looked out behind the yacht. "Yeah, of course."

While he ducked below deck to grab his things, I dropped anchor and pulled over the sun visor. Stuart came back up, vest gone, towel draped over his arm, and the bottle of sunscreen in his hand. He held it out to me. "Would you mind?"

I took it and rolled my eyes. "It's not exactly a hardship."

He chuckled and turned around, giving me his back. I applied sunscreen, covering his back and the nape of his neck, rubbing his shoulders, and even giving him a little massage. "You're not so tense today," I said.

"Imagine how relaxed you could get me," he said, his voice low. I dug my thumbs into the knot of his shoulders, intending it as a jab to what he said, but he moaned instead. "Jesus, your hands..."

I dropped them and took a small step back. "You're done."

He turned to face me, his imploring gaze full of mischief. "Would you mind terribly doing my front? I'd hate to get sunscreen on your yacht."

I stared at him. And Jesus, he was being serious.

"I don't think that's a good idea."

He looked around the cockpit. "I know. That's why I asked. I'd hate to get sunscreen on your seat or your ladder when I hold on."

I fought a smile. "That's not what I meant."

"Oh, I know." He sighed dramatically. "Well, if you won't do it for me, could you watch me do it and point out any parts I miss? I'd hate to get sunburnt." He dropped his towel onto the seat and made a show of pouring sunscreen onto his palm. How could he make that sexual? God, it may as well be honey, or lube, or any-fucking-thing I'd like to lick off him.

And as if that wasn't bad enough, then he rubbed it all over his chest, his abs, down below his navel... and his eyes never left mine. His tongue peeked out at the corner of his mouth, and he stretched his neck and rubbed one hand over his throat while his other hand slipped just under his

Speedos. It made me look at the bulge barely concealed by his swimmers. "Did I get everywhere, Foster?"

I swallowed hard and forced myself to make eye contact. "You were pretty thorough, yeah."

One corner of his mouth rose in a sexy-as-hell smirk. "I've been told that before."

My nostrils flared. "You don't play fair."

He shook his head slowly. "I'm not playing."

Fuck.

Sure, it was summer, and sure it was the tropics, but that had nothing to do with the sweat that beaded all over my body. I let out a shaky breath and reached up to a line of sunscreen he'd missed under his eye and smeared it with the pad of my thumb. I wanted to slide my thumb across his lip. I wanted to slip it into his mouth, let him suck on it...

"Join me," he whispered. "You know you want to."

I knew exactly where we'd end up if we got into the water together. "I was going to make a start on an early lunch," I replied. There was no conviction in my voice, and he knew it.

He leaned in and whispered in my ear. "I'm not hungry for food." Then he turned, collected his towel, which he dropped near the ladder, and dived into the water.

I all but collapsed onto the seat, taking in deep breaths. I wiped my forehead, my face, and felt my heart hammering in my chest. Jesus, Lord have mercy, he was going to kill me.

I shouldn't encourage this. I should have told him when this whole playful flirting thing started that it was a no-go. I had rules in place for a reason. I had a business, a reputation.

I also had a hard-on that wasn't going away any time soon.

I had urges and desires that I hadn't wanted to act on

with anyone else. Then Stuart Fucking Jenner boarded my yacht and everything went to hell.

I should go down to the galley and prepare some lunch. I should turn on the TV for a distraction, or read a book, or go into my bathroom and take care of my aching dick, thinking about anything but him.

Him in the water, just a few metres away. Him, with the come-fuck-me eyes, who wants me to join him—and not just join him in the water. Him, with the scorching hot body who's offering himself to me. Him, yes him.

I should not want him. I should not want this. And most of all, I should not get into the water with him. I knew how it would end. I would dive into the water with him, and he'd swim over to me with that devastating smile, and he'd reach out for me and I'd pull him close. He'd wrap his legs around me and I'd tread water, holding us both up, and he'd crush his mouth to mine. I'd finally get to taste him, to have that gorgeous pink tongue of his in my mouth, and then we'd bring it on board. On the deck, on the cockpit seat, down in the cabin, on the floor, on the table, in his bed, in mine.

"Fuck."

I stood up, pulled my shirt over my head, took two long strides, and dived headfirst into the water.

CHAPTER SEVEN

STUART

I DIDN'T THINK he'd cave so easily. I thought he might fight a bit harder, but no. He dove into the water just by me. His strong, tanned body cut the water like a knife. He surfaced and turned to me, shaking the water from his hair, sultry and hot, and even a little pissed at himself. "Happy now?"

I grinned. "Oh yeah. Water's nice, don't you think?"

He stared for a while, then leaned back in the water, bringing his legs up, sunning his chest. "Water's perfect."

His eyes were closed and he was smiling, looking relaxed and totally at peace. I envied him that. I envied him a lot of things. I floated like he did, closing my eyes to the sun, warm and dreamlike, and I could have almost fallen asleep if it weren't for him laughing beside me and splashing water at me.

I started, getting upright, and splashed him back. "What was that for?"

He was grinning and squinted at the sunlight. "You looked too relaxed."

I grabbed his shoulders and tried to push him under, but

he barely budged. He took a hold of my waist, and my legs instinctively went around him. He froze at first, then he relaxed and his eyes glinted with something I hadn't seen before. I rolled my hips against his chest knowing damn well he could feel my cock, and I leaned down, just about to take my lips with his when a motor sounded close to the yacht.

We turned to see a small boat come around on the other side of us, and Foster was quick to push me off him. He gave me a parting apologetic glance before swimming back to the yacht, then pulled himself up the ladder and waved to the passing boat. I took my time paddling back and hoisted myself up the ladder, not particularly caring that my dick was half-hard. Foster, who now had a towel hanging around his neck, was checking something on one of the screens, so I stood on the back deck and dried my hair.

He glanced over at me, took in my shameless bulge, then met my eyes. He tried not to smile and turned back to the screen. "You know, most people wouldn't be concerned with covering their hair."

I glanced down at my barely concealed cock tenting my swimmers, looked back at Foster, and shrugged at him. "I'm not most people. And anyway," I held my arms out and turned side to side. "I work hard on this body. I'm not hiding it. I'm not *used* to hiding it."

Foster straightened up and gave me an appreciative once-over. His smirk grew sly and one eyebrow raised slightly. "Thought you'd wear more suits than anything else."

"In the office, yes. In the clubs and on weekends, hell no." I slung the towel over my shoulder, making no attempt to hide my crotch. "Well, shirtless mostly. But I'd love to work on my all-over tan."

"I, uh," he started, his gaze darting to the other boat that was now anchoring within waving distance. "I'm not sure they'd appreciate the view."

I stepped into the cockpit and sat on the long seat, my legs sprawled. "Or they could love it."

He watched me for a long second, shook his head a little, and turned away. So, we were back to avoiding... Two steps forward, one step back. I didn't mind. I had eleven more days to play this game.

"So, um, lunch? I could grill some chicken to have with a mango salsa. How does that sound?"

"Perfect. Where my biggest decision is whether to snorkel or sunbathe before or after lunch. Or vice versa." I sighed and stretched my arm out, maybe flexing my abs a little. "What do you suggest?"

He licked his lips; his voice was gruff and sexy. "It'll be too hot to lay about in the sun after lunch, so I'd suggest sunbaking before, snorkelling after."

I smirked and looked him over, head to foot. Was that a bulge in his board shorts? "Will you snorkel with me? I could use a guide in the water. And if you wanted to join me lazing about on the deck in the sun, working on getting rid of tan lines, I wouldn't mind."

He barked out a laugh. "Oh, I'm sure you wouldn't."

I made a point of looking at his dick, then smiled right at him. "Something tells me you wouldn't mind either."

Just then, another boat sailed onto the same reef we were on, taking both of our attention. It was like a metaphorical bucket of cold water for Foster; I could see it. His eyes hardened, focused like it reminded him this was his job, not some sex cruise. I sighed as the offending boat stopped on the other side of us, again within waving distance. The soft mutter of voices carried over the breeze. "Is it always so busy out here?"

Foster nodded. He was now holding his towel in front of his groin, kind of casually, but it told me our little flirting game was over. "Yeah, during the day. These guys'll be gone mid-afternoon."

"Good." I frowned. "I kind of liked being out here alone."

He started. "Oh, we can find another reef if you want? There are plenty, but this little atoll is one of the prettiest."

I considered saying *yes, take us somewhere more secluded*, but there was no rush. And the other boats were far enough away, and this atoll was gorgeous. It was no wonder other people wanted to be here too. "No, it's fine here. They don't bother me."

"Okay, good." He seemed relieved by this. "Just let me know if you want to move on and we will. I um, I'll make a start on lunch."

"And I'll make a start on my tan lines."

He chuckled and quickly descended the stairs into the cabin, so I took my towel and walked up on deck, around the side, and up to the bow of the yacht. I'd never seen water this clear or this colour before. The ocean floor must have been four metres down, but I swear I could see every grain of white sand. The glare off the water and off the white boat was kind of harsh, and I regretted not thinking to grab my sunnies. I threw my towel out and laid down. The warmth of the boat felt good; the warmth of the sun felt great. I closed my eyes to the glare and lowered my swimmers over my arse, snorting with the realisation that the glare of my white arse cheeks could probably blind someone on a passing boat.

I could get used to this. I briefly wondered if it was

called *defecting* to simply never go back to real life... I wondered who would actually miss me... I wondered how busy my office was at that very second and realised how much I didn't care. How much I didn't miss it, surprised me.

I snoozed with a smile.

The tropical sun was baking me, and I could feel it restoring me, refilling my almost-depleted energy levels in ways I didn't know were possible. In ways I didn't know I needed. I could feel the stress leaving my body, my muscles relaxing, my mind clearing. And I could also feel my arse burning, so I rolled over and sunned my front, pushing my Speedos down as far as public decency allowed. I considered taking them off completely, but I didn't fancy Foster getting into trouble should someone report him back to his head office. So I cinched them down a little further, almost tucking my dick down between my legs to reveal as much skin as I could.

Of course, my dick liked being handled, shoved and confined in tight spaces, and started to fill slowly.

I lay back enjoying the languid, sexual sensations that stirred in all the right places. Enjoying the sun, the heat on my skin, the rock of the yacht. It felt like I was being watched, and I wondered if the people on one of the nearby boats were enjoying the view... Until Foster cleared his throat. "Um, sorry to interrupt."

I opened my eyes, squinting up at him. "Don't be sorry."

His lips twisted into a pouty smile. "Lunch is ready."

I leaned up on my elbows so I could look down my body. Yeah, my dick looked happy to be snug and confined. I spread my thighs a little. "I might dive in to cool off first if that's okay. I'm working up a sweat."

Foster's nostrils flared. "I can see that. In fact, everyone out here can see that." He waved absently toward the other boats.

I stood and picked up my towel, not fixing my swimmers, not fixing the way my dick was pulling the white fabric downward, revealing neatly trimmed hair and the stalk of my cock. "Like I said, I'm not used to hiding," I said as I brushed past him. "And if they don't want to see, they shouldn't look," I added as I walked along the side deck to the back of the yacht. I dropped my towel and dove into the water. It was so cool against my heated skin, it took my breath away.

And it fixed the elongating problem in my Speedos too.

It was probably just as well. I was so horny, at this rate I'd be in my room all afternoon jerking off, so the cool water tamping down my libido wasn't all bad.

I climbed up the ladder, only fixing my swimmers when I picked up my towel. I roughly dried my hair, making it stick up everywhere, no doubt, then tied the towel off around my waist.

Foster watched the whole show. He was particularly fascinated with a bead of water that ran from my nape, over my collarbone, and down my chest. "You know," he said, licking his lips. "Towels are for drying bodies too, not just hair."

"I like to let the salt dry on my skin," I replied as I stepped down into the cockpit. Foster had put the tray of food in the middle of the bench seat. There were two plates full of salad leaves, sliced grilled chicken, topped with a mango salsa. I sat down and picked up a plate. "This looks amazing."

He was still standing where I'd walked past him, like he was in a trance and my words broke the spell. He shook his head and sat down. "Oh, thanks. Dig in."

I took a mouthful of everything, and oh, my God. "Which family member do I have to thank for this?"

He shot me a puzzled, amused look. "What?"

"Which family member? The prawn dish was your aunt's; the salad dressing last night was from your dad. Who'd you steal this one from?"

"No one." He grinned. "Okay, well, I saw it on some cooking show, but I customised it."

"Well, you outdid yourself. Holy shit, this is good."

"Thanks." He relaxed a little then, smiling as he ate. "How was the water just now?"

"Perfect. Everything here is perfect."

He nodded slowly. "I'm glad."

"So, will you come snorkelling with me after?"

He glanced at me quickly before studying his plate. "Maybe."

I grinned. Now, I was a clear believer in no meaning no and yes meaning yes, and I knew that hesitance always landed squarely on the no side, but damn. That maybe, his maybe, with those smouldering eyes and the way his gaze raked over my body, the way he licked his lips and groaned real quiet, was almost a yes. But it was a hesitant yes, so I would wait for him to make his move.

And it had to come from him.

I'd put my cards on the table. Laid them out for all to see. Hell, I'd basically offered myself up on a freaking platter. I'd clarified if he was single, if he was interested, if he was willing...

He just needed to establish himself as player two in this game.

"So," he said. "Do you have family?"

I nodded and swallowed my food. "Yep. Mum and Dad,

divorced when I was nine. One sister, Dana, two years younger than me."

"You guys close?" He made a bit of a face, like he knew these were personal questions but he couldn't stop himself from asking.

"Yeah, I guess. We all still live in Brisbane. Catch up when we can. What about you? I'm guessing with the recipe swaps that you're all pretty close."

He chuckled and stabbed some salad with his fork. "Yeah. When I was a kid, my cousins were my best friends. Mum's got three sisters that she's close to, so I kind of grew up with four mothers. Mum and Dad have been married forever, and I have one sister and one brother." He shoved his fork in his mouth and chewed thoughtfully. "We're all kind of scattered now, but we still try and call every other week. We have Christmases together no matter where we are in the world."

"Have they taken advantage of you having the best job in the world and demanded free week-long cruises around the tropics?"

He laughed, making little lines crease at the corners of his eyes that did some weird swooping thing to my belly. "I offered."

"Did you snorkel with them? Or is it just me who will get special treatment?"

He shoved another forkful of food in his mouth before his smile could become a grin. "I haven't said I would yet."

I let my fork slide out slow between my lips. "You will."

He laughed me off, shaking his head as he finished his lunch. "You know, there's better snorkelling spots further northeast. I mean, it's good here, but it depends on what you're after. Coral or fish."

I shrugged. "I don't care, to be honest. I just want to try it."

"Try it? You've never snorkelled before?"

"When I was like ten. Though I don't think the mechanics of it will have changed too much."

"Well, no..."

I gave him a sly smile. "But you better come snorkelling with me, just to be sure."

"You really don't take no for an answer, do you?"

"Not often."

He put his empty bowl on the tray and sighed. "Then I better get the gear ready."

I took the tray and headed down to the galley, Foster fast on my heels. "You don't have to wash up," he said, looking horrified.

I put the bowls in the sink and gave him a smile. "Are you going to argue with a customer?"

"Stuart," he tried again. "I cook and clean; you relax. That's the deal."

"Well, you cook; I clean. That's the new deal," I said. "If you let me cook dinner, then you can wash up."

"This isn't... that's not how... Stuart."

I matched his tone. "Foster."

He sighed, and I saw his need to look after me warring with his belief to not argue with a paying client. I kept washing up, ignoring him standing there watching me. "Oh," I added as if I just remembered. "I'll need you to help with some sunscreen before I go back in the water."

He half sighed, half growled. "You're kind of infuriating, you know that?"

I nodded brightly. "Yep. I'm a lot of things. Infuriating is just one of my many talents."

He rolled his eyes and walked up the stairs, presumably

before he said something he probably shouldn't say to a client. I chuckled as I finished washing up, and by the time Foster came back into the cabin, I had everything dried and put away too.

He looked at the tidy kitchen as though it pained him to see it. "Thank you," he said quietly.

"You're very welcome."

He chewed his bottom lip and waved his hand to the stairs. "I have all the gear ready up on deck, so whenever you're ready..."

I grinned at him. "Oh, I'm always ready. Let me just grab my sunscreen."

CHAPTER EIGHT

FOSTER

HE WAS GOADING ME. And teasing and flirting with zero shame. He smirked. He licked his lips, sliding his tongue out provocatively. His eyes were full of heat and dare. I was in a permanent state of semi-arousal around him, as though my dick knew where it wanted to go.

At least my board shorts hid it, not like his goddamn Speedos.

He went up the stairs first, so of course I got an eyeful of his arse, which did little to help the problem in my boardies. He looked around the scenery, noticed another boat off in the distance, then handed me his sunscreen and turned his back to me. "If you don't mind."

"I don't think you'd care if I did."

He laughed. "I'm not opposed to shoulder massages, either."

I squirted a line of sunscreen along his shoulders and began to rub it in. "So, infuriating and insufferable are both talents you're proud of?"

"Yep. Infuriating, insufferable... insatiable."

I dug my thumbs into his shoulders, hard. But instead of hurting him, he moaned like he loved it. "Incorrigible."

He dropped his head and chuckled, and as I rubbed further down his back, he groaned. "Jesus, you're really good at this."

"So I've been told." I squirted more sunscreen onto my hand this time and palmed his shoulder, his nape, the tops of his arms, and he was moving with my touch. Pushing back against me, falling into me. Receptive, pliable.

When he turned around, he was also turned on. His eyes were closed, so I rubbed sunscreen over his chest, and when my hands trailed down over his abs, a smile tugged at his lips. But his eyes stayed closed, so I allowed myself to look. Being this close, I could see how his nipples pebbled, how his skin moved under my hand. How he angled his head when I ran my hand up his neck, his eyes closed, his lips slightly parted.

He was beautiful.

I wanted to kiss him. He'd let me. Hell, he'd welcome it. But I had no doubt if we kissed right now, it wouldn't end until we were naked and sated. The sexual tension between us was like a stick of dynamite, just waiting to explode, and once the fuse was lit—and we were going to light it; it was only a matter of time—it would be one helluva detonation.

I pulled my hand off him and it took him a few seconds to open his eyes. "Why'd you stop?"

I held out the sunscreen. "It's my turn."

One corner of his mouth pulled upward, a filthy smirk that tightened my balls. "Thought you'd never ask."

I turned around so he could do my back, and he drizzled the sunscreen across my shoulders and began to rub it in. It felt so good; his hands were strong, certain, rubbing in slow circles, pushing and pulling me. I could just imagine what he'd be like in bed...

Goddammit.

"Want me to do the front too?"

I bit back a moan and seriously couldn't have said no if I'd wanted to. I turned to face him, ignoring his sly smile as he rubbed cream over my chest, my stomach. "Don't think this means anything," I said.

He chuckled. "Of course not. Sun safety is very important." His eyes said nothing whatsoever about sun safety. He gripped my chin, swiping his thumb along my jaw. "Though you do look particularly hot with white cream smeared next to your lips." My mouth fell open, making him grin. "Don't be so shocked. It doesn't mean anything."

I stepped back, and my dick protested. "Snorkelling," I said, ignoring how hoarse my voice was. Ignoring how his Speedos almost didn't contain his erection. Ignoring my own aching cock.

Ignoring how the sexual tension ratcheted up another notch.

I made myself walk to the back of the yacht, and I made myself pick up the mask and snorkel. I made myself take some deep breaths, which was useless because he was soon standing beside me. He was holding the snorkel and mask, and I was waiting for a comment about using spit to defog the mask, but thankfully he didn't. He was actually serious and listened to my instructions and safety spiel with no jokes, no innuendos. I was grateful that he took it seriously —took my job seriously—and wasn't a jerk about it. He knew when to play, and he knew when not to, and I really liked that.

So, with flippers and masks on, and mouthpieces in, we stayed near the yacht until he was more confident with the breathing. And in what felt like hardly no time at all, he could dive right under and blow the water out his snorkel without inhaling any water. We dove down to the bottom, the water crystal clear, the sand immaculately white, and he pointed excitedly when he found something new. A fish, shells, coral, he was amazed by it all. His whole face lit up, smiling around his mouthpiece, and if I'd had any doubts about joining him snorkelling, I was so glad I did.

It was amazing, and it was a joy for me to experience it with him. Gone was the smug, corporate type, and in his place was a guy who was in awe of his surroundings. He looked younger, happier, even more gorgeous.

And mind you, seeing him swim, dive, and glide underwater in those tiny white Speedos wasn't exactly a hardship.

All too soon we were back at the yacht, and I wondered which version of Stuart would get out of the water. The finance guy, who flirted and acted all sexual to stop people from seeing the real him? Or the guy who let his guard down, who I'd just spent two hours with in the water, smiling with abandon and having the time of his life?

He threw his mask and mouthpiece on board, hoisted himself up so he sat on the platform near the ladder, and pulled his flippers off. He was breathing hard, but his grin was huge. "That was the best thing ever."

I sat next to him and pulled my flippers off as well. "Yeah, it was."

"Can we do it again? Somewhere else? Where there's more fish and coral?"

His excitement was contagious. "Definitely. We can head around to the east of this reef if you want. It'll have what you're after."

"Cool. When?"

"Now, if you want."

He shrugged. "Maybe later, or tomorrow? I'm beat right now. You must be too."

I conceded with a nod. "Snorkelling can be hard work."

"Oh, hey," he said, looking out over the bow. "One of the boats has gone."

This made him happy, clearly. "If you want to go somewhere more private, you just have to ask. This reef is a popular stopover because it's so beautiful, but I know a few other spots that are just as good and not so popular."

"I don't mind other people being around. Out there." He gave me a nudge with his elbow. "But I gotta say, I'm glad it's just us two here."

Before I could reply, his stomach growled. He patted his tummy. "And apparently snorkelling is good for the appetite."

I laughed. "Yep. Come on, I'll grab us a snack."

"Need me to clean up our snorkelling gear?" he asked as we stepped into the cockpit.

"I'll take care of it," I said. "It's fine."

"Or," he countered, "you can show me how to do it so I can do it next time."

I tied my towel off around my waist. "There's absolutely no point in me arguing, is there?"

He grinned and rubbed his towel over his hair. "Nope." He slung his towel over his shoulder, making no attempt at covering his now wet and very see-through swimmers.

"You do know those Speedos are see-through when they're wet, right?"

He laughed and didn't even look down. He held my gaze like a dare. "Yes. It's why I bought them."

I snorted quietly. "Figured." I couldn't help but smile at him. "Righteo, snack first, then we clean the snorkelling gear."

We demolished a platter of fruit, cheese, and crackers, then true to his word, he wanted me to teach him how to clean and store the snorkelling gear. Which led me to teach him how to check and store the safety gear, which led to me teaching him how to use the radio, how to activate the distress beacon, how to call for help, and how to talk to other vessels nearby. Again, he was studious and serious, listening and only asking questions if he wasn't sure.

He was so easy going, so carefree. So different from how I imagined he would be in a boardroom. Much like myself. He still had some dark circles under his eyes, though his face had some colour now; whether that was purely from the sun, or if it was because he was unwinding, I wasn't sure. He sure looked a lot happier than he had just yesterday. He was standing up on the deck, arms out in the hot afternoon breeze.

"You know what we should do?" he announced.

I was almost too scared to ask. "What's that?"

"We should put the sails up and see where the wind takes us."

I squinted at him. "Really?"

"Yes." He gave a hard nod. "Absolutely. Let's just go wherever and find somewhere new."

"Wherever the wind takes us?"

He jumped down into the cockpit, renewed energy in his eyes. "Yep. Except if it wants to run us aground. Or into a reef or another boat. But you know what I mean. Throw caution to the wind, live a little, do something spontaneous."

I grinned at his enthusiasm. I highly doubted he got to do anything remotely spontaneous. "Okay. You're the boss."

His whole face lit up. "Really?"

"You remember how to pull up anchor and set the mainsail?"

He was beside himself with excitement, and he leapt into action. Fifteen minutes later, we were sailing, and his grin couldn't possibly get any wider. Evidently, the wind was taking us northeast, which was kind of perfect. Once we were out of the shallow reef, Stuart was behind the wheel watching the bow. I clapped him on the shoulder. "You've got this under control. I'll go make a start on dinner."

He gawped at me. "You can't leave me out here driving by myself!"

I waved him off. "You're not driving. You're sailing, and you've got it covered. Give me a holler if you're going to hit anything."

His mouth fell open, and I laughed as I took the stairs below deck. We were barely cruising at four knots in calm water. This side of the reef was protected from open water, and all he had to do was keep the reef on our starboard, the mainland on our port side, and he'd be fine.

If I doubted him for one second, there's no way I'd have left him. But something told me he needed this. He liked control, he liked testing himself, he liked proving himself. He liked to be challenged, and conquering this would be good for him. I knew that having a mid-career crisis meant a world of self-doubt and a crushing sense of failure. He needed something he could master, especially with the whole 'throw caution to the wind, living a little' speech earlier, he needed to do this on his own.

I sliced and marinated some lamb, made a Greek-inspired salad, stocked up the fridge with beer and water, and tidied up a bit. Then, "Ahhh, Foster? Hey, Foster?"

I dashed up the stairs. "What's up?" I asked, looking around for any immediate problems.

"There's a boat." He pointed over the bow to a tiny white dot on the horizon.

God, he was being serious. "Yes, that's a boat. Actually, that looks like a ship."

He was alarmed. "Could we hit it?"

I tried not to smile. "If we stayed this course and maintained this speed, then yes. In about ten hours." Then I laughed. "Stuart, it's miles away."

He shot me a look. "Yes, well, how was I to know that? You just left me here!"

"And you did a marvellous job." I didn't really have the heart to tell him his steering was probably the equivalent of my dad letting me reverse the car out of the garage when I was fifteen. It was technically driving but had nothing to do with road rules, driving at speed, navigating dangerous conditions, or how the vehicle handled and reacted.

"What about this reef here?" he asked, pointing up ahead. "Looks like a good place to stop."

"Perfect," I said. It was right in between the Elford and Moore reefs, and the currents were good. "Okay, bring her around starboard. Nice and slow."

With his eyes trained on the bow, he eased the wheel and steered us in safely. Perfectly. "Now, wind the sail in," I ordered.

He jumped up and had the lines in in no time while I took the helm. He was adept on board. Most people were wary of footing, holding on to anything bolted down. But not Stuart. It was like he already had a feel for the yacht, her movement in the water, his balance and spatial awareness in relation to her movement.

When he had the sail rolled in and came back to the wheel, grinning. "Can we drop anchor here?"

I nodded. "It's sand below us. It's fine."

He released the anchor, then straightened up and gave me a worried look. "Sand... Of course, we can't just anchor anywhere. It'd damage the reef."

I smiled at him. "Exactly. I have a special anchor that minimises damage, even on sand. By law you can't drop anchor on protected reef areas, but I wouldn't anyway." I walked to the back of the yacht and motioned for him to join me. "See? It's just sand here. The anchor is fine; there's plenty of swing room. Can't damage anything. See those white pyramid buoys floating further in on the reef? They're like a no parking zone."

He looked out, nodding slowly. "So we can stay here tonight?"

"You picked a perfect spot."

He smiled but was soon serious again. "What other rules are there to protect the reef? What can and can't you do? There have to be rules, right?"

"Lots of rules."

"But that's a good thing, yeah?" He frowned. "Because it's dying, isn't it? The reef. I'm sure I read something about coral bleaching."

I nodded. "Humans certainly haven't done it any favours. But there are a lot of people working on conservation, restoration. Even understanding how coral behaves, how it lives, how it dies. Only time will tell if we can win the race to save it."

"That's kinda sad, isn't it?"

I nodded. "For sure. We just need to make sure we do little-to-no damage at all."

He looked me square in the eye and said, "Over dinner, you can tell me everything I should be doing, even at home in Brisbane, to be more aware. Like products that end up in waterways and all that kind of stuff."

So I did.

I grilled the lamb while he set the table in the cabin, and we talked all things eco. He surprised me by what he already knew, but true to Stuart's form, he listened, learned, asked questions. I thought I would have bored him to tears, but our conversation never stopped while we ate. It was rare for me to find someone I was on the same level with, and again, I was glad his friend had decided not to come with him. I know that made me selfish, but I just couldn't seem to care. It also made me horny.

Knowing he was willing and had offered for me to take the friend with benefits option put my dick on edge. It had been a long time for me, and being so close to him didn't help; this trip was by far the most intimate I'd ever had.

The fact he was still wearing nothing but his tiny swimmers didn't help either.

Neither did the fact that he devoured his dinner and moaned with every mouthful, licking his lips and humming in appreciation. He wasn't trying to be sexy or even playful —I'd seen that whole production to know the difference— this was just Stuart being himself without anyone else around to judge him.

He was letting his guard down with me, and that was the biggest turn-on of all.

He stacked his empty plate on top of mine and slid them onto the sink. "I had no idea lemon went so good on lamb salad," he said, taking the small plate of sliced lemon. "You know what would go even better with lemon? Beer or tequila."

"There's both. You can pick."

"Will you have one with me?" he asked, not really giving me any time to answer. He took two out of the fridge in one hand, grabbed the plate of lemon with his other. "Come on, let's go watch this sunset."

He was up the stairs to the cockpit before I could argue. Which, with Stuart, I was soon learning was a waste of time. I followed him up to find the two bottles on the bench seat with the plate of lemons and Stuart nowhere in sight. I heard a splash and a laugh, so I ran to the back of the yacht to find him in the water, grinning up at me. "Come in with me," he said. I tried to think of a valid reason to say no, but he wasn't having any of that. "I'm the boss, remember?"

I sighed, pulled off my shirt, and dived headfirst into the water beside him. I broke the surface to see his smiling face, his hair slicked back, and possibly the happiest I'd seen him yet. He swam over to me, put his hands on my shoulders, and tried to dunk me like he'd tried before. I grappled with him and easily shoved him under, which I think might have been his ploy all along because, when he grabbed hold of me again, he wrapped his legs around me.

He came up grinning, his hair flattened against his fore-head, water beading down his face, and he bit his bottom lip. He had his legs around me, I was holding him up, and he was looking down at me. I was barely keeping my head above the surface, treading water, and he was so close he could have kissed me.

I thought he was going to. I wanted him to. I could feel his cock against my belly and mine responded in kind. Like he knew that, he unhooked his legs and pushed off me and swam to the ladder. With a flirty look over his shoulder, he hoisted himself up the stairs, his body bronzed in the setting sun, perfectly sculpted, dripping wet, and yep... those damn white Speedos.

By the time I climbed the ladder, he met me on the deck

with both bottles of beer and he handed one to me. He'd poked a slice of lemon into it. "Cheers."

I tied the towel off around my waist, hopefully hiding my semi. He was killing me with the push-and-pull game he was playing, and I wasn't sure how much more of it I could take. I took the beer and followed him into the cockpit where we sat side by side on the bench seat. "Thought a quick cool off was in order," he said, taking a swig of his beer. "It's still hot and humid, even as the sun's going down."

"Well, it is the hottest time of the year in Far North Queensland." I took a mouthful of beer and was pleasantly surprised by how refreshing it was. "Man, this is good." I turned the Corona over in my hand; I'd had hundreds of these. I wasn't sure what made this one in particular so good. Maybe it was the heat, the humidity, all the exercise we'd done swimming, all the sunshine. Maybe it was the man sitting next to me. I wasn't sure if it was his body heat I could feel or the rays of the setting sun.

He took another mouthful and sighed, stretching his legs out. His towel was around his waist, but of course it was open at the front. He had no shame. "I could stay here all night," he said. "This is utterly perfect. Look at that sunset." It was true. The sky was a golden orange over an aqua-coloured ocean. It was gorgeous.

After a moment of silence to appreciate the end of the day, he started talking about Brisbane, his job, what he loved, what he hated. If it were a pro/con list for his internal debate about quitting, it wasn't a contest. I didn't mind him venting to me; I understood. I really did. I had been in his shoes, literally. Same industry, same job, same dilemma. And listening to him speak freely showed me an insight to the real Stuart Jenner. He was passionate, honest, driven.

Eventually his tirade ran out of steam, and he looked a little lighter, like his burden had lifted a little. I had to wonder if he'd made a decision.

Another two beers and the sun was gone, but the lights in the cabin were enough and the light of the moon on the water was something special. We'd talked about everything from professional surfers to the sustainable palm oil industry in Sumatra, and I was a little buzzed from my three beers. I couldn't deny my attraction to him. Not just physically, but he was smart and concerned about politics and the state of the world.

And the more he talked and laughed, the more I liked what I saw. The push and pull between us had become one steady push. It wasn't a matter of will he, won't he. It was now just a matter of when.

He'd been all over me in the water, and now sitting beside him, our shoulders almost touching, he would sometimes brush my thigh with his hand when he talked, and it sent a warm buzz through my veins every time. Every time he smiled, every time he laughed, every time he looked at me.

"You know what we need?" he asked.

"What's that?"

"Well, a lot of things," he said, grinning. "Some cabin boys. Some eighteen-year-old twinks. Do ships still have cabin boys?"

"I don't think so." I snorted. "And we're not a ship. We're a yacht."

"Same thing," he dismissed me. "But you're missing my point."

"Well, no, I got your point. But I can't help with the twinky cabin boys."

"You don't seem to want to help me at all," he said with

a nudge of his shoulder. "I all but offered myself to you and you said no."

"I didn't technically say no..."

He stared straight ahead. "You didn't say yes either." Then he sighed and changed his tone. "And that's fine. I can take a hint. You want to be in my arse, but you have those business ethics that prohibit fraternisation with clients. I get it." He waved his hand. "Good work policies are... honourable, I guess."

I opened my mouth to speak, to tell him I... I wasn't sure what I was going to tell him. But my mind had taken me to the gutter as soon as he said I wanted to be inside his arse, and I was stuck there. Visual prompts and filthy fantasies took hold of all reasonable thought.

He stared at me then for a good long second. "You know what we do need?" he said, standing up and disappearing below deck. He appeared a second later with a bottle in one hand, two lemons in his other. "Tequila."

I snorted out a laugh. "My favourite cocktail mixer. A shot of tequila with a dash of good intentions and you have a cocktail aptly named 'What the Fuck Have I Done?'."

Stuart laughed as he trudged up the stairs. His towel was long gone; just his tiny scrap of swimwear remained. "Well, two What the Fuck Have I Dones? coming right up."

He sat back beside me and held up the bottle. "What even is this?"

"*Alquimia Reserva de Don Adolfo Extra Añejo*," I replied. "The world's best tequila. Goes down easy, so be careful."

He gave me a sultry grin. "Oh, believe me. I love things that go down easy." I rolled my eyes, but he laughed as he quartered the two lemons on the plate. When he was done, he took the lid off the bottle and a piece of lemon. "Lick, sip, suck. You game?"

"Do I have a choice?"

He chuckled. "Well, you do. But I can see in your eyes what you want. You just need a little Mexican courage."

I looked at the bottle and then the lemon he was holding. "You don't have any salt."

His voice was rough and he grinned salaciously. "Oh yes, I do."

Then he leaned in, and licked up my chest to my neck. I was stunned, speechless, and he laughed, took a small swig of tequila, then sucked on the lemon. He shook his head and breathed through the burn of alcohol and sour lemon.

"Oh, that is good," he said. I didn't know whether he was talking about licking the salt off my skin or the tequila. "Your turn."

He shoved the bottle in my hand and held out a piece of lemon. I was done with the push-and-pull game. I was done with not touching or tasting the platter of man on offer in front of me. I could still feel the burn of his tongue on my skin.

I took the lemon, but I held it up to his mouth. "Open."

His pupils dilated, his nostrils flared. *Oh, he likes being told what to do.* Then he parted his lips, just enough for me to slide the lemon in. I leaned right in, almost pushing him backward so I was over him, and I licked from his collarbone to the edge of his jaw. The salt on his skin from the ocean, from the humidity, was tangy on my tongue. He moaned as I licked up and nipped the angle of his jaw with my teeth. I took a quick swig of tequila, then held the back of his head and took the lemon from his mouth.

It was a tangle of salty lips, sweet tongues, and sour lemon. It was the most delicious kiss I'd ever had.

I pulled back with the slice of lemon between my lips and slowly drew it out of my mouth. He was panting, his lips wet, his chest heaving, his cock hard across his hip, barely confined in his Speedos.

He snatched the bottle from me, took a piece of lemon, then stood up and straddled me.

Oh fuck.

He tilted my head back while he slipped the lemon into my mouth. Then he licked my neck, my shoulder, my ear, swallowed a mouthful of tequila, then tried to pry the lemon out from between my lips. But I wasn't surrendering it easily. I gripped his hips and bucked up against him, and he gripped the back of the seat in one hand, my jaw in his other.

"Give it to me," he growled.

The lemon? My cock? I wasn't sure at this point, but at that moment, I'd have given him anything he wanted. I relinquished the lemon and he sucked it into his mouth while grinding down on me. His cock was fully erect, peeking up from under the elastic of his Speedos with every roll of his hips.

Fuuuuuuck.

Then he stopped still, leaned back a little, and said, "Lick my abs."

Doing exactly as he instructed. I trailed my tongue up his stomach to his sternum. He tilted my head back and poured a quick drop of tequila into my mouth, then took the lemon and squeezed it over his nipple up to his collarbone.

Fuck yes.

I lapped at the lemon juice, flicking his nipple with my tongue. He arched his back and I held him while I licked and sucked his pebbled flesh. He rolled his hips, searching for friction, and his rock hard cock slid out of his swimmers.

My mouth watered.

"Stand up," I ordered.

He slowly put one foot down, then the other, and I pulled him between my spread knees. His cock was glorious; veined, uncut, and tanned like the rest of him. I held the base of it in my fist and took him straight into my mouth.

Stuart fisted my hair, pulling tight and guiding me with long, deep strokes. He sure wasn't timid about demanding what he wanted, and it was hot. My cock was aching but I ignored it for now, making him my one and only focus.

He moaned while I worked him over. "Fuck yes," he bit out. "God, that's good." He thrust into my mouth, deeper into my throat. "Holy shit."

I swallowed around him and he tried to pull out, as if that was the only warning he could give me, but I gripped his arse and pulled him all the way down. He groaned long and loud as he came, pulsing down my throat. He thrust a few more times, then, trembling, he pulled out, unsteady on his feet.

With a bit of a laugh, he went to his knees in front of me. He looked blissed out, his eyes glazed over, a sated smile on his face. I leaned back, letting my hips slide forward a bit, and slowly undid my board shorts. I pulled my hard-on out of my briefs and hissed at the contact. I was so turned on. I'd been in a state of semi-erection all fucking day, and this was going to border on painful.

Stuart looked up at me like he was starving, and in one movement, he licked me from base to tip and took me into his mouth.

I was never going to last long.

He pumped and sucked me, and the second he groaned around me, my orgasm dropped on me like a bomb. I came so hard, I almost blacked out. Ecstasy exploded deep in my belly and fired pleasure along every cell as he sucked me dry.

Fuuuuuuuck. He had one helluva talented mouth.

When he pulled off, he licked his lips victoriously, very much the cat who got the cream. "Well, it's official," he said, grabbing the bottle of tequila. "Lick, sip, suck is my new favourite game."

CHAPTER NINE

STUART

I TUCKED my dick back into my swimmers and fell onto the seat beside him, half leaning on him, our bodies touching from shoulder to foot. Feeling a little drunk and a lot brazen, I slung my leg over his thigh and offered him the bottle of tequila.

He put his hand up and let it fall heavily on my thigh. "No thanks. I've had enough."

"I probably have too," I admitted. "And I don't have any more lemon up here, and I've done you, so I'm all out of things to suck. Unless you're good to go again."

He barked out a laugh and pulled up his swimmers, tucking himself away. "Not immediately, no."

It wasn't a hard no. I sighed happily. "Today has been incredible. Not just tonight and not my amazing dick sucking skills, or yours I might add, but the whole day." My words were getting a little slurred. "I'm considering defecting. Kinda like *The Hunt for Red October*, but instead of having Russians, submarines, and Sean Connery, we have Aussies, yachts, and you."

He patted my leg. "If this was like *The Hunt for Red October* and you were defecting, you'd be Sean Connery."

"Shit. Well, okay. You are quite correct," I said in the best Sean Connery accent ever.

He laughed. "Okay, that was bad. You sounded like Billy Connolly trying to do an Australian accent."

I squinted one eye at him, trying to focus. "How come you're not drunk?"

"I'm used to Alquimia."

I held up the bottle. "It's good tequila."

Smiling, he took the bottle and stood up, then he took my hand and pulled me to my feet. "You need to be in bed."

I slid my hand around his back, pulling us flush together, and gripped his arse. "Thought you'd never offer."

He laughed. "I wasn't offering."

"'S probably just as well," I said. "I'm a little drunk."

"Just a little?" He was still smiling at me.

"I do accept rainchecks though."

He helped me down the stairs, then into my room. "I'll see you in the morning."

"Yes, you will," I replied, aiming for my bed. I stopped, remembering I was still wearing swimmers. "Oops, these are not pyjamas." I pulled them down and stepped out of them, letting Foster get a good look at me completely naked. He'd just had my dick in his mouth, so I figured we were past modesty. And look at me, he did. Smiling, I knelt on the bed, aimed my head toward the pillow, and fell forward.

"That's not pyjamas either," he said. He sounded a little gruff, or maybe I was just drunk.

I opened my eyes to see him still standing at the door watching me, so I rubbed my arse cheek. "If you want to fuck me, I won't stop you. In fact, just having a dick in my arse gets me off."

He stepped toward the bed and I went warm all over, thinking he was going to do what I wanted. He could so easily kneel on the bed, straddle me, pull down his shorts, and bury himself inside me. Instead, he pulled the blanket over me. "Goodnight, Stuart," he said, walking out and closing the door behind him.

"Party pooper," I mumbled, but he was already gone.

I CRACKED ONE EYE OPEN, saw that it was daylight, and ran a manual checklist over my body. Stomach: okay. Head: okay. Confident I'd survived relatively unscathed, I sat up and did another stocktake.

Even with the gentle rocking of the boat, I actually felt half decent. I looked down at myself, saw I was naked as the day I was born, and I groaned. Then I remembered stripping in front of Foster and offering him my arse. Which he'd declined... but I *was* drunk. *Damn him and his upstanding morals.*

I sighed and scrubbed my hands over my face, resigned to apologising to him, and then I remembered the blowjobs we'd exchanged on deck last night. I smiled as I remembered the look on his face, how he sounded, how he tasted...

I rolled out of bed, found my Speedos on the floor and pulled them on. I adjusted my dick, which was half a hard-on, half a piss-on, relieved myself in my bathroom, brushed my teeth, and freshened up. It wasn't enough to wake me up, and all I really wanted to do was dive off the back of the yacht.

I opened my door to find the cabin empty and headed to the cockpit. Foster was lying across the bench seat reading something on his iPad, but he sat up when he saw me. "Oh, here he is. Good morning! How are you feeling?"

"Me: one. Tequila: zero. Except I don't know what time it is, and if I don't dive into the water right this second, I'll need to re-evaluate those statistics."

He laughed and waved his hand toward the ocean. "Be my guest. I'll get you some breakfast." When I got to the back, just before I dived in, he said, "Oh, and Stuart?"

I turned to face him. "Yeah?"

"It's seven fifteen." Then he looked me over from head to foot and back up again. "And I'm glad to see you forgot where the rest of your wardrobe is."

I looked down and readjusted my dick, more for his benefit than mine. "You're welcome."

His laughter was the last thing I heard before I went headfirst into the water. It was cool, fresh, and everything I needed. I could feel it fixing me before I even broke the surface. There truly was something medicinal about saltwater. I floated on my back for a while, enjoying the sun on my face and the way the water lapped at my ears, and by the time I climbed the ladder and boarded the yacht, I felt great.

Foster came back up into the cockpit as I was drying off. He held a plate and a cup of coffee. "For you."

My stomach growled like it was trying to eat its way out of my body. "Oh my God, is that a bacon and egg sandwich?"

"Sure is. Figured you might appreciate the grease, salt, and protein."

I took the plate and raised one eyebrow, leaving the protein jokes unsaid. From the way he kind of blushed, I didn't have to say it. But I was glad things between us weren't awkward. "How long have you been up?" I asked, taking the coffee he offered and sipping it.

"Since six."

"Sorry about last night," I said, getting it out in the open first up.

He flinched a little before he schooled his reaction. "Which part?"

"Stripping naked in front of you and inviting you to fuck me," I said, taking a bite of my sandwich. It was absolutely divine. "Oh my God, this is good," I mumbled with a mouthful of food. Once I swallowed it down, I added, "The offer still stands, just so you know, but I shouldn't have put you in that position. Oh, and I'm not apologising for the whole tequila lick, sip, sucking dick thing because I'm not sorry that happened. At all."

His smile became a chuckle, his cheeks pink. I think my forthrightness surprised him. "I'm not sorry either. As long as you're okay with it."

I washed a quick bite down with coffee. "I'm very okay with what happened last night, and I'll be happy with it happening every night. Or day. But me stripping and planting myself in bed and saying what I said was a bit out of line. So I'm sorry."

He nodded slowly, and it looked like he was trying not to smile. "It was... informative."

I took another bite and shrugged as I chewed. "And it was also true."

Now he laughed, but he changed the topic. "How's your breakfast?"

"Amazing. Just what I needed. Between the bacon, caffeine, and a quick dip in the ocean, I feel great."

"Good."

"What're our plans for today?" I asked, finishing my sandwich.

"I've put through an order to be picked up from Port

Douglas the day after tomorrow, so we'll have to head further north at some point. But what we do in the meantime is up to you. What did you want to do?"

"Swimming, snorkelling, sunbaking, maybe a nap."

"Sounds good."

"Then after we've dropped anchor tonight, we can do more shots of tequila."

He let his head fall back and groaned. "We'll run out of lemons at this rate."

"That's okay. As long as we have the lick and sip sorted out, we can find something else to suck."

He covered his face with his hands and mumbled, "You have no shame."

"None." I drained my coffee. "And from the look of that smile you're trying to hide, I think you don't mind one bit."

He let his hands fall away and gave me a scorching look. "I thought it was pretty obvious last night that I didn't mind one bit."

I chuckled, but I knew what was coming. "And here comes the *but*..."

He cocked his head. "What?"

"The part where you say, 'It was fun and all, *but* it can't happen again.'"

He made a face and looked out over the water. "There was no but. Not from me. Although it should be said that I shouldn't be fraternising with clients, but I think we're past that. But," he said the word slowly. "I won't push. If you say no more, then there's no more."

Hell fucking yes.

I fought a smile. "I'm not sure how to say that," I pretended to concentrate really hard, "Nnnnnnoooooo mmm... How did you say that again?"

He smirked and sounded it out slowly. "No more."

I tried again. "Nnnnoooo mmmm..." I shook my head. "Just can't seem to get my mouth around it."

He rolled his eyes, grinned, and stood up. "I have some work to do. I'll leave you to your sunbaking or whatever you want to do first."

"Oh, that reminds me," I said, standing up in front of him. "I'm going to need help with the sunscreen again." I gave him a waggle of my eyebrows. "If that's okay."

He chewed on the inside of his lip and stared at me for a long second. "Can't have you getting sunburnt now, can we?"

I shook my head slowly. "Nope. And later, before you join me for a swim and snorkel, I can return the favour."

He made a low grunting sound that curled low in my belly, before disappearing into the cabin and coming back up with sunscreen. I figured if I was being all flirty and suggestive, I may as well play hard. "How do you want me?" I asked, turning to kneel on the bench seat with my hands up on the deck. I looked over my shoulder to find him smiling and shaking his head, so I stuck my arse out a little more. "Like this?"

"You are trouble," he said, pouring sunscreen into his hand. He smeared his palm across my shoulder and down my back, hard and sure, and just as I lowered my Speedos down my arse a little, another boat came puttering around the atoll. "Oh, what a shame," he said sarcastically. "Prying eyes make for good behaviour."

I chuckled. "Or an appreciative audience."

He laughed again but didn't say anything more; he just rubbed cream into my back and when he was finished, he leaned in close, pressed himself against my arse and said, "All done."

Hot pleasure sank through to my balls, but he stepped

away and laughed when I groaned. "You're a cruel man," I called out as he went down into the cabin. His laughter echoed up at me.

"You give as good as you get," he yelled back.

I readjusted my cock and groaned again. But I couldn't be mad. I'd spent two days teasing him. Hell, I'd just knelt on the seat and stuck my arse out at him. I grabbed my towel and went up to the deck on the front of the yacht and sprawled out. It was hot already. Barely eight-thirty in the morning and the sun was scorching.

Considering there were other boats around, I couldn't sunbathe naked, so I pulled my Speedos up my arse crack to expose my cheeks to the sun. I pulled them down at the top a little, making the fabric as small as I could, then spread my arms out and closed my eyes.

I could have easily fallen asleep, and maybe I did doze a bit. It was relaxing as hell, perfect in every way. My real life in Brisbane was just a thousand kilometres away—it may as well have been on a different planet.

I could forget about the pressure, the deadlines, the budgets, the interest rates, the global economy, the stress. I could feel the sun working its magic, dosing me up with vitamin D. That made me snort. With a bit of luck, I'd be getting a different kind of vitamin D later tonight.

I rolled over to sun my stomach and again, pushed my swimmers down to get some colour over my tan line. Then something Foster said came back to me.

We were stopping at Port Douglas, and I had a day tour booked to go into the Daintree National Park. When I'd booked the holiday, I figured a day hiking on solid ground through the world acclaimed rainforest, with Jason, would be a nice change from sailing.

Now I'd be going alone, which wasn't all bad, though I

had to wonder if Foster wanted to join me. It was booked and paid for after all, for two people. Would he think I was crazy? Pushy? Clingy?

Lonely?

I sighed.

I didn't want to be overbearing in any way, and I had no doubt he had plenty to do on the mainland without playing babysitter to me. But who knew... maybe he never got the chance to go sightseeing because he was always busy or maybe because he was never asked if he wanted to join in. And it *was* just the two of us. It wasn't like he had anyone else to look after. Plus, he clearly wasn't opposed to spending time with me.

Well, not physically anyway. He was all for sex for as long as I was. It was up to me to say no, which was never going to happen.

He was hot as hell, had a gorgeous dick, strong hands, and a talented mouth.

God, his tongue, his tongue...

Just thinking about his mouth had me getting all hot and bothered again, and it had nothing to do with the summer sun. So, I took my towel back to the stern, dropped it by the ladder, and dived into the water.

It was a blue I couldn't quite identify. I think the word cerulean probably covered it but still didn't do it justice. The reef was so pretty, so beautiful. I truly understood why Foster chose to come here when he walked away from the rat race.

If I ever had the balls to do that, this is where I'd come too.

That realisation—that I would never have the guts to do what he did, that I was bound to the life I had back home—

left a heaviness in my chest that startled me. It was a sinking feeling that squeezed the air out of my lungs, which wouldn't have been so bad if I was on dry land. But I wasn't. I was swimming by myself in the open ocean. I swam back to the yacht before the squeezing got any worse, before the heaviness dragged me under. I grabbed hold of the ladder and caught my breath, grateful Foster wasn't out here with me.

Was that a panic attack? Or the beginning of one?

Jesus.

I did as my doctor had taught me. Deep breaths, repeated *I am in control* on a loop through my mind a few times, and slowly climbed out of the water. I'd had moments like that before, but never when I was in the water. The crushing feeling I could barely manage when breathing oxygen became a whole different game when not on dry land.

I tied my towel around my waist, sat on the back of the yacht with my feet in the water taking calming breaths until I felt the squeezing recede. I was fine. I was safe. I was in complete control. I could hear Foster talking to someone on the radio, confirming a mooring by the sound of it, and his voice helped calm me.

Or maybe knowing I wasn't alone calmed me.

Because back home, even surrounded by hundreds of people, associates, colleagues, I was always alone. But out here I wasn't. It was quite ironic that in the open vastness of the Coral Sea and the Pacific Ocean, I'd never felt more not-alone.

I shook my head and let out an almighty breath, stood up, and approached the cabin. Foster was on his radio, a clipboard in hand, checking off some list, and he gave me a surprised smile. He clearly wasn't expecting to see me so soon. I clapped my hand on his shoulder to acknowledge him, but I walked straight into my room and closed the door.

I showered and hung my swimmers over the rail to dry, pulled on some underpants, and crawled back onto my bed. I just needed some space and time to get my head around what had just happened. A niggling thought in the back of my mind told me I should call my doctor and tell her I'd had an episode while swimming alone in the ocean; I could have found myself in real trouble if I hadn't been so close to the yacht. Maybe that was a little over dramatic and I was completely over-reacting. Or maybe it was so close to the truth it scared me.

I rolled over and found my phone but couldn't bring myself to switch it on. I dreaded the hundreds of emails, missed calls, text messages and voice messages that would no doubt bombard me as soon as I turned it on.

Instead, I slid my phone back onto the bedside table, pulled the sheet up over my hips, and closed my eyes.

A SOFT KNOCK on the door sometime later woke me. A little drowsy, I looked up to see Foster poke his head through the doorway. "You good?"

I sat up. "Yeah." My voice was rough and I scrubbed a hand over my face and through my hair.

"Your hangover must have snuck up on you," he said, but there was concern in his eyes.

"Nah, I'm all right," I replied. I looked down then to see the sheet was covering most of me, though it was very clear I was wearing red briefs and nothing else. "What time is it?"

"Midday." He opened the door fully now and leaned

against the jamb. "I just thought I'd check to see if you were okay. You looked a little pale when you came in. You've got some colour now though."

"Yeah, I feel good now," I said, not openly admitting to feeling off before. "What's for lunch? Need me to help you with it?" I scooted off the bed and stood there, wearing nothing but underpants.

Foster gave me a once over and smirked when he met my eyes. "Red Calvins today? I'm not exactly disappointed, but I was getting used to the white Speedos."

I found myself smiling at him. "I rinsed them in fresh water. But don't fret. They'll be back on later. Or I could just wear these all day." I looked down at myself.

He smiled as though he rather liked that idea. "Oh. Your lunch is ready." He turned and went back to the galley, and I reluctantly pulled on some shorts. When he saw me, or rather, when he saw I actually had clothes on, he did a double take.

"Disappointed?" I asked.

He handed me a plate. "Maybe."

"You can take them off me later." I looked at what he'd made us for lunch. "This looks really good."

"Taco salad. It's not exactly healthy, but it has lettuce."

I inspected my plate. "And beans and tomatoes and cheese. It totally counts. And exactly what I feel like, thanks."

"I thought you might have been a little hungover..." He studied me for a second. "Nothing like tacos to fix you right up."

"You want a water?" I asked, opening the fridge with my free hand. I handed him a bottle of water, then took one for myself. We went up to the cockpit and sat on the bench seat. I looked out across the reef. "Do you ever get sick of that view?"

Foster laughed and shoved a forkful of tortilla chip and salsa in his mouth. "Never."

"Get sick of me asking you that?"

He snorted and chewed his mouthful. "Nope."

"It's bloody hot today though." I could already feel sweat on my brow, running down my back. "Is it going to storm or something?"

Foster glanced up at the very blue, very cloudless sky, then looked at me like I was mad. "It's just humid. You sure you feel okay?"

I shovelled a huge mouthful of salad into my mouth, taking some time to chew and answer. "I feel pretty good. Just a bit tired still. Nothing a swim and another nap and a few shots of tequila won't fix."

Foster laughed as he ate, then nodded to my water. "Just make sure you stay hydrated."

"Yes, Dad."

His smile made his eyes gleam like sapphires. "I'm not old enough to be anyone's dad, let alone yours."

"Oh, come on, you're a smoking hot daddy."

He burst out laughing, and I decided right there that I needed to hear that sound a whole lot more. "Well, they don't call me that to my face."

I chuckled and we finished our lunches in companionable silence. It was nice. Just us, the entire Great Barrier Reef, miles of ocean, and several other boats dotted around us. I drank half the bottle of water in one go, realising maybe I was a little more dehydrated than I realised. "Tell me, what will you do while I'm on the rainforest tour?"

He shrugged. "I'll stay on board."

"Doing what?"

"Cleaning, restocking, grab some fresh food."

"Don't forget more lemons."

He cleared his throat, trying not to smile. "And limes."

Now it was me who burst out laughing. I nudged his foot with mine. "If you want to chase your tacos with a shot or two, I'll happily immerse myself in the ocean so you have some salt to lick."

He smiled but gave a small shake of his head. "One mustn't swim directly after eating. Water safety, one-on-one."

"Well, I'm all for one-on-one."

He took my plate. "I'll clean up after lunch. You take it easy." As he went down the stairs, he said, "And you can't swim in those shorts."

By the time he came back up, I was lying down on the bench seat with my shorts hanging over the steering wheel. My red Calvin briefs would pass as swimmers to any passing boat. Foster baulked when he saw me but soon smiled. "That's not really what I meant."

I closed my eyes to the sun. "But you don't mind."

"Hmm," he murmured. I could feel his eyes on me, like warm fingers instead of the sun. "If we're going swimming or snorkelling, I'll need some help with sunscreen. If that's okay."

I opened my eyes, and yep, there he was staring at me with the sunscreen in his hand. "We must be sun-smart, mustn't we?"

He gave me a sly smile. "We must."

He tossed the sunscreen to me and peeled off his shirt, laying it on top of my shorts over the wheel. I looked point-edly at his shorts. "And you can't swim in those."

He chuckled, and surprising me, he undid the button and fly and pulled his shorts down. He stepped out of them, standing there wearing nothing but black briefs. His bulge hung snug in the material; his body saw more sun than he let on. "I think you sunbake naked."

He laughed. "Not when I have clients on board."

"So if I go swim for a bit, will you strip completely naked and lie down on the deck?"

He snorted out a laugh and looked over at the closest boat. "Pretty sure there's laws against it."

"There are no laws against being naked on private property."

"It's not the nakedness they'd mind," he said, low and delicious. "It's how it would end when you came back from your swim. On the deck. In full view."

I stood up and poured sunscreen onto my palm, standing in front of him. I was pretty sure he had a semi. I stepped around him and rubbed his shoulders with the sun cream, probably standing closer than was completely necessary. "Sounds like you've given that some thought," I murmured. "Any preferences?"

He huffed out a laugh and leaned into my hand. I rubbed his shoulders, down to his lower back, then walked around to his front, making sure he was covered. Yep, he definitely had a semi. "I'm not one for... exhibitionism."

I rubbed sunscreen over his chest, down his arms, over his abs, carefully watching what I was doing and enjoying him watch me do it. Then when I rubbed a little lower, down to the elastic of his briefs, I watched his eyes instead. "I can wait for the sun to go down." My gaze fell to his lips, then back to his eyes. And man, there was fire in them now. I leaned in just enough to speak against his lips. "Come swimming with me. I want to be able to lick the salt off your body."

His breath caught and his eyes burned with want. "You enjoy this game, don't you?"

"What game is that?"

"The chase. Being relentless until you get what you want."

"I'm good at it."

"Yes, you are."

"But I don't always get what I want, when I want it," I said, my lips almost brushing his. "Because right now I want to kiss you so bad."

"Why don't you?" he breathed the words.

"Because you said we need to head north today." I took a step back and smiled as he almost fell forward. "And if we start anything now, we won't be going anywhere."

He shook his head, breathless. The distance between us, barely a metre, seemed to give him enough clarity. "You're probably right."

"I still want you to swim with me though." I handed him the sunscreen and turned my back to him.

He smeared sun cream over my back, and his voice was warm on my shoulder. "Why's that?"

I could hardly tell him the real reason, that I'd almost had a panic attack in the water before and I was kind of freaked out by it. "Because I don't want you jerking off up here without me."

He laughed. "Is it possible to die from blue balls?"

I chuckled. "I think it might be. But don't worry, if you pass out, I'll be sure to give you mouth to... mouth."

He groaned, and he was now standing so close, I could feel the heat from his body, and I knew I was probably taking things too far. I mean, games were fun and all, but I didn't want to be cruel. So I turned around, took the sunscreen, and poured a little onto my fingertips. I swiped gently across his cheeks, down the bridge of his nose, finishing with a *boop* on the tip. Then I quickly slathered my face, and when he'd finished rubbing his face, I took his hand and led him to the back of the boat. I could see the ladder was down, so, still holding his hand, I said, "Ready?"

And we jumped.

CHAPTER TEN

FOSTER

WE PLAYED AROUND in the water, floating and laughing for a bit, then Stuart grabbed the snorkel gear and we swam for what felt like hours, diving down to look at the reef and the fish.

It was so perfect, and I had to keep reminding myself he was a client.

A client who, I had no doubt, I would be having sex with later that night. As far as sexual tension went, we were now off the Richter scale.

He was back to his grinning self, bright-eyed and enthusiastic about everything he found under the surface. At one point, a fish startled him, and I laughed so hard I had to pull up to the surface for air. He followed up and pulled off his mask just to tell me to piss off and splash me, but he was smiling.

And his demeanour now, his happiness, was vastly different from how he'd been this morning. He'd kind of played it off as being a bit hungover, but I doubted that was it. He'd been pale when he went into his room for a while, and it hadn't looked like a hangover to me. There'd been something in his eyes that told me otherwise. So I'd left him alone, thinking he just needed some downtime, but by lunchtime, he still hadn't come out, so I knocked on his door. I hadn't thought he'd be asleep. As soon I realised he was, I pulled back, but he stirred.

The sheet was covering him, though I could see a partial thigh and hip. He looked peaceful for that briefest second. And absolutely beautiful. Then he sat up, the sheet tangled around his hips, his hair was kind of mussed, and he squinted and scratched his head.

It was adorable.

I'd wanted to climb into bed with him and muss him up some more.

Same when he climbed up the ladder into the yacht before me. I got a glorious view of his arse in those red briefs, and when he met me at the top, he handed me a towel. He scrubbed his towel over his hair, making it stick up all over. His smile was devastating.

And those red briefs were pretty spectacular dry, but wet? I wanted to meet Calvin Klein and kiss him.

"What are you thinking?" he asked, a curious smile in his eyes.

"That Calvin Klein is a genius."

He looked down at himself, then back up at me and grinned. "Mr Klein can't take all the credit."

I snorted. "No, he can't."

He laughed too, then looked out across the reef and sighed. "Are we on the move again? Should we pull up the anchor?"

"Yep. You wanna be in charge again?"

His smile became a smirk. "I'm always in charge. But if you mean do I want to be the one behind the wheel, then no. You can drive this time. I'll sit and watch the master at work."

"Always in charge, huh?" I countered. "That's not what you told me before."

He tied his towel around his waist, sat down, stretched out, and crossed his legs at his ankles; relaxed and comfortable. "No, I said I liked to be fucked into the mattress, but that doesn't mean I'm not in charge."

I barked out a laugh. "If you say so."

He put his head back, closed his eyes to the sun, and smiled. "I can show you later."

My dick perked up at his words, but I let the subject drop for now. He was right; we did need to move. "Come on, look alive," I said, patting his shoulder as I went past. He opened his eyes as I stepped up onto the deck. "I'll get the mainsail. You get the anchor."

Not long after that, we were sailing. I was behind the wheel, but he sat with me, watching our course, checking our depth, and as always, asking questions.

We headed north and set a steady pace toward the east side of Arlington Reef. It was tourism central, even on a bad day, and there were plenty of boats around. But the winds were on our side, and if I needed to change tack, Stuart held the wheel and listened to every instruction. It was a solid few hours sailing, but I wanted to shelter inside the horseshoe of Arlington Reef, behind Oyster Reef for the night. The water would be calm, we could drop anchor in the sand without worrying about reef damage, we could snorkel, swim, then grill some steak.

Oh, and have shots of tequila and lick the salt off each other's bodies.

Yeah, let's not forget that.

Stuart's face when we were sailing, though, was pure

joy. As soon as we caught the wind, we cut the water like a knife, and it felt like we were flying, and his smile could have lit up the entire eastern seaboard.

He lifted his fist into the wind and let out his freedom cry of "wooooo" and it made me laugh. And it restored his energy, because when we finally dropped anchor, bright-eyed, and right or wrong, he wanted to do everything. "A swim before dinner," he suggested. "We can snorkel the reef, even walk in the shallows if we can."

I checked the time. "If we're quick."

He disappeared and came back fifteen seconds later with our snorkel gear in his hands and a grin plastered on his face. And half a minute later, we were snorkelling. Arlington Reef was popular for good reason: it was spectacular. Most of the Great Barrier Reef publicity photographs were taken here. There was even a permanent pontoon where charter boats could stop and let the flocks of tourists off.

We kept our distance from that. Stuart didn't have to say he preferred privacy—I saw disappointment on his face every time another boat came within a cooee. The reef itself was huge and we'd picked a remote spot, so in the waning afternoon sun, we were on our own.

And he was a pro at snorkelling underwater now. Stuart's grin got wider with every different thing he saw: the fish, the coral, the stingrays, the turtles. He'd mastered the whole diving down thing, and he even understood my hand signals.

Being with him like this was special. I rarely got any personal time, and even though this was technically a job and he was my client, it didn't feel like it. I felt as though I was on holiday, that I was showing a friend the reef for the very first time and we had the entire Coral Sea to ourselves; just him and me.

It felt incredibly personal.

And as we made our way back to the yacht, I was trying to come up with valid excuses why that was a bad thing.

I couldn't think of one.

Next week, he'd be going back to his life in Brisbane, and I'd be picking up my next charter tour. Life would go on. So why not just enjoy this for what it was? Why not think of this week as a paid holiday?

Stuart certainly wasn't opposed.

And from the ache in my balls and my permanent semi, my body wasn't opposed either.

"Here," Stuart said, taking my snorkel mask. We'd just climbed back on board the yacht and I'd barely finished wrapping my towel around myself. "I'll go clean these. You start dinner, and when I'm done, I'll get us a drink."

"Oh, right," I said. "I forgot, you're in charge here."

He shot me a grin over his shoulder as he went about his business. But, I did as he suggested, and when he came below deck, he was only wearing his red underpants; his towel was gone. He noticed that I noticed. "Towel's drying in the sun," he said. He looked down at my crotch. "Want me to take yours?"

"Not right now," I answered. "I don't fancy cooking whilst semi-naked." I also didn't fancy pulling the towel away to reveal the semi-problematic semi I was sporting.

"Fair enough." He looked around the galley. "Where can I cut some lemons?"

I put the steak on the griddle pan, waiting for the sizzling sound to settle before I spoke. "Isn't it a bit early for lick, sip, suck?"

He grinned. "I was actually going to grab some beers

first, but if you want to start with the hard stuff, I won't say no." He licked his bottom lip and his eyes gleamed with mischief. "I bet we're covered in salt. Might take a lot of licking."

I tried not to smile too hard. "Lemons are in the fridge; cutting board in the cupboard next to the sink. And a beer'll be fine."

He found everything he was after, then sliced up a lemon while he talked about the incredible turtle we'd seen while we snorkelled. He marvelled at the magnificence of it all, shaking his head like he couldn't believe what he'd seen before he grabbed two beers from the fridge, popped the lids, slid in a lemon slice, and handed me one.

"Do you ever get complacent with it?" he asked, taking his first sip. "Do you ever just think, 'Meh, seen it all before'?"

"Never." I shook my head and turned the steak. "You can't take that for granted. I don't take any of it for granted. Not the reef, not the weather, not this job, none of it. And anyway, no two trips are the same. It's different every time."

He took a swig of his beer. "How so?"

"Well, I might come to the same reef, but the sunsets are never the same. The people I bring out here are never the same."

"Ever have a client you considered throwing overboard?"

I smiled and sipped my beer. "Nope. I've been pretty lucky. Had some language barriers, but smiles are universal. And funnily enough, so is the theme music to Jaws."

He burst out laughing, but then he asked, "Have you seen many sharks?"

"Oh, sure. Most are harmless, but not all of them." I turned off the griddle plate and dished up some leafy greens and potato salad. "Sharks are just an occupational hazard. Some idiots used to try and get real close to stingrays too. Until Steve Irwin. Now they respect them a bit more."

He nodded slowly. "I bet they do. Ever had any client try and take coral?"

"Once. Now I make sure they know the rules. People are pretty good about it." I slid our plates onto the table and we took our seats.

"This looks really good, by the way," he said. "Thank you."

"You're welcome."

"I'm surprised by how hungry I am. I mean, back home, I never eat snacks, and I certainly wouldn't eat carbs like this," he said, shoving a piece of potato salad in his mouth. He hummed his appreciation.

"You'd be surprised how much energy you burn by swimming and snorkelling." Then I added, "You don't need to worry about your diet out here."

"Well, carbs are my enemy. But protein," he said, waggling an eyebrow. "Now shots of protein are always on my menu."

I rolled my eyes. "Then the steak will do you good."

He laughed, and we ate the rest of our meal talking about what was going on in the world. He cleaned up the galley after dinner, and I went up to the cockpit to double check everything was good for the night. When I walked along the deck by the coach housing, he was coming up from the galley with a plate of cut lemons in one hand, the bottle of tequila in his other. "Dessert is served."

I let my head fall back and groaned, and as soon as I was back in the cockpit, he handed me the bottle. "Don't be a spoilsport." Then he looked out over the ocean at the setting sun, and more specifically, at the lack of other boats. "Oh, would you look at that... everyone's gone. That means we can play this game out here." He handed me the plate of lemon slices, stepped right in close, kept his eyes on mine while he bent down and licked from my nipple to my throat, sending a shiver right through me, then took a swig of tequila. He shoved a piece of lemon in his mouth, shuddered, and grinned. He shook his head and groaned. "Man, that's good."

He was still only wearing his red briefs. I could see how good he thought it was.

"Your turn, but first," he said, then pulled at my towel, revealing my underwear and that damn semi-hard-on I'd had all day. "Mmmm. That's so much better," he whispered. Then he held a slice of lemon between his teeth and held his arms out wide. "Lick me."

So I did.

I licked along his collarbone, took the tequila bottle and had a swig, then opened my lips and slid the lemon piece into my mouth. He surrendered it quickly, gripping the back of my neck and kissing me, the lemon going from his mouth to mine.

He didn't wait for me to catch my breath. He licked up my neck to my ear, sucking the lobe between his lips, then pulled off to sip the tequila. I could barely even think straight, let alone get a piece of lemon for him. He grinned and, pulling out the elastic of my briefs, popped a slice of lemon so it stuck out the top, just below my navel. "Oh my, would you look at that," he said gruffly before sinking to his knees. He knelt before me, his hands on my hips, and nudged his nose to the ridgeline of my cock in my underwear, then snagged the lemon between his lips and pulled it out.

The cheeky fucker.

He tongued the lemon, and keeping it in his mouth, he then rose to his full height. His eyes locked on mine, full of heat and dare. I was done with games. I pushed him so he sat on the bench seat, his surprise quickly dying as I took his nipple in between my teeth. He arched his back, jutting his hips forward, searching for any friction I could give him.

He snatched the lemon out of his mouth. "Oh fuck," he cried out when I rolled his nipple between my teeth. He gripped my face in both hands and brought me up for a kiss. Our mouths locked, tongues twirled and tasted. But it wasn't enough, our bodies couldn't touch like this. It was nowhere near enough.

So I pushed him, gently urging him to lie down along the bench seat, and he pulled me down with him. We were a tangle of limbs and tongues; I was leaning over him, our cocks aligned, our chests, our mouths. My God, he could kiss.

He roamed his hands over me, my back, my arse, grinding me on top of him. It was kind of awkward, not an ideal position, but I was too turned on to stop. If I pulled away now, it might very well kill me.

Then he slid his hand between us, and after a little fumbling, he had our cocks in his fist. Sliding, slick with precome, and it was magical.

So, so good.

"Oh fuck, you feel amazing," he whispered, his voice barely a breath. Then he groaned and bucked his hips like he was close.

I crushed my mouth to his, and he took my tongue, moaning and pumping, and it was all too much and far too good. I fucked his fist, his cock hot and hard against mine, slick and slippery, and so fucking good.

I broke the kiss so I could speak. "I'm gonna come."

"Fuck yes, come on me."

I pulled back, and we both looked between us, our cock-heads slipping through his fist, over and over, and my orgasm crashed over me. Pleasure rolled through my body, sweeping and all-consuming, and I shot come onto his chest and belly. His grip tightened as he came, his pulsing cock milking the last of my orgasm from me as his come pooled with mine on his skin.

He shuddered and shivered, then let out a pained laugh. "Holy fucking shit," he mumbled.

Unable to stay upright anymore, I fell forward, smearing the mess between us, and buried my face into his neck. He smelled of the ocean, of sex, of us, and I inhaled for all I was worth. "You good?" I finally asked.

He chuckled again. "Very."

I nuzzled in and closed my eyes despite the odd angles of my legs. "I should get you cleaned up," I whispered. "Don't know if I can move though."

"We could just jump in the ocean," he suggested. "I would say we could shower together, but there's no way we're both fitting in the showers on this boat."

I pushed up off him, my boneless body protesting every movement as I stood. "The ocean it is then."

He looked directly at my cock, hanging half-hard from my briefs, then up at my belly and chest to where our come now covered my skin. "Fuck, that's beautiful."

I chuckled, a little embarrassed, but then I noticed his cock was poking out of his briefs, his belly covered in our come. We were lit only from the lights in the cabin, and it gave him a warm glow. "Yes, it is."

He grinned, stood up and pulled his underpants down, and stepped out of them. "What?" he answered my questioning look. "It's completely dark. No one can see us."

Not as game as him, I tucked myself back in but jumped into the ocean with him. Only when I surfaced, he quickly found me, wrapped his arms around my shoulders, his legs around my waist, and he kissed me.

I couldn't tread water for too long, and as we began to sink, we broke apart laughing. "I should swim naked more often," he said, grinning. The moonlight made his teeth gleam.

"Except that fish might mistake you for a tasty sea worm. Especially at night."

His eyes went wide and he swam for the yacht, but my laughter must have given me away. He took hold of the ladder in one hand and splashed me with his other. "Not funny."

Except it kind of was.

I followed him out of the water, not before I watched his glorious naked arse in the light of the moon. Water beads shone like diamonds as they ran down his body, and I wanted to catch them, taste them... He thrust my towel at me, distracting me from staring at his naked form. "Like something you see?"

I patted my face and held his stare. "You know I do."

His lips curled up on one side, and he stared for a long second. Then, abruptly, he looked out over the water and dried himself before tying the towel around his waist. He was covering himself, protecting himself, and I knew he was about to ask me something that left him vulnerable.

He did this every time.

When he was on show, when he was luring something he wanted, he'd proudly show off his body, suggestively leaving his semi on full view in his Speedos or briefs. But as soon as something became personal or he felt vulnerable—like he did when he asked if I was seeing anyone—he covered himself up. Apparently modesty went hand in hand with his vulnerability. I wondered if that was why he was so ruthless in a boardroom; his expensive suit was an armour. But here, and right now, he was exposed. He shook his head and gave me a tight smile before he turned to go into the cockpit.

I grabbed his arm. "Did you want to ask me something?" I prompted.

"Nah, it's okay."

"Sure?"

He nodded, so I let his arm go. He stepped down into the cockpit and picked up the bottle of tequila. He held it up in one hand, the lid in his other. "Want another drink?"

I snorted. "No. I need water."

His smile was back. "Me too."

We went down into the cabin and I pulled the door closed behind us. Stuart put the tequila back in the liquor cupboard, then grabbed two bottles of cold water and handed one to me.

"Thanks," I replied. "So, you've got a day on the mainland tomorrow."

He nodded slowly and took a long pull of water from his bottle. "Yeah. I've never been to Trinity Beach or the SkyRail. Heard it's pretty cool. Have you been?"

"Not for years. It's amazing. You'll love it."

He nodded again, an odd expression on his face. "What will you do while I'm away?"

He'd already asked me that... "A bit of cleaning, do some laundry, restock the fridge. You know, all the fun stuff."

He took another long drink of water, his Adam's apple sliding up and down in the most distracting of ways. Then he gripped the sink behind him and I wondered if he was off balance, but no, it seemed he was steeling himself.

"You could come with me? Do the day tour through the rainforest. Then we can get whatever food we want at the markets. I'll even buy you dinner and have you back on board by nine o'clock tomorrow night."

If I was going by his voice alone, his couldn't-care-less tone, slight shrug of his shoulder, I might have thought it was a throw-away invitation. But his cheeks tinged pink, and his knuckles were white where he gripped the sink, and he held his breath waiting for me to answer.

Two things were very clear to me in that moment. One, it wasn't often he asked people questions he didn't already know the answer to. And two, this question, this invitation to spend the day with him, was not just an invitation to spend the day with him. It was more than that. To him, at least. It was him making himself vulnerable, wanting something he wasn't fully prepared to admit to wanting. He was afraid of rejection; he was scared I'd turn him down. It was pretty obvious he didn't put himself out there very often, and I wanted to know why.

I met his gaze and saw the fear of failure in his eyes, the fear of finally finding the courage to ask for something he wanted, only to be told no. The fear of putting your heart on the line, only to be laughed at.

So, Mr Hotshot Corporate Finance Guy was only human after all. There was a chink in his perfectly polished armour. He might think it was a flaw, but to me, it made him better. There were layers I wanted to peel back, explore.

This was becoming more than just a holiday fling. We were going from friends with benefits, to something else. It was feeling more like my pretend boyfriend on vacation fantasy every minute.

Did I want to spend the day with him on the mainland? Hiking, shopping, going out for dinner? Hell yes, I did.

I didn't care that my smile might give me away. "Sure."

My answer shocked him. "Really?"

I walked over to him, leaned my body flush against his, and kissed him. No tequila, no water, no games. I put my hand to his face and deepened the kiss, teasing his tongue with mine. A long kiss. Heavenly minutes we stood there, holding each other, tasting each other. I ended the kiss, only to kiss him again, soft and sweet, before pulling away. "Yes, really. Sounds great. We'll need to set sail for port pretty early though."

"So you're saying I should be a good boy and go to bed early too," he asked, his lips wet and plump. "And alone."

"Oh, yeah," I answered, stepping back. "If I take you into my cabin, we won't be going to the mainland tomorrow."

He licked his lips and smiled, his eyes going from my mouth to my eyes. "But tomorrow night?"

I let out a breathy laugh and had to make myself walk away, or I would take him into my room. Fuck, he was so sexy. "Goodnight, Stuart."

His huge grin was the last thing I saw before I closed my door.

CHAPTER ELEVEN

STUART

I WAS UP EARLY—JUST before six—thinking we could make a head start, but I found Foster at the wheel in the cockpit and we were already sailing. Which would explain the rocking of the boat. "Oh, morning," I said, taking the stairs into the cockpit. "I thought it felt rough. I wondered if the weather had changed."

"Morning," he replied with a grin. "And no, we're cutting across the water, heading west to the mainland. It's not too rough though."

I looked out at the water. It was smooth enough, but we were going against the grain, if you will. "You were up early."

He grinned as he steered, not taking his eyes off the bow of the yacht. "Yeah, have an important day trip with this hot guy planned. Don't want to be late."

I rolled my eyes to dull my smile. "Whatever."

He laughed. "No, I want to get moored while the tide is in."

That seemed a more Foster thing. "Want me to start breakfast?"

He glanced at me. "You don't have to..."

"I can make toast," I grumbled, going back into the cabin. Yes, I was his client, but it *was* just the two of us. I could also help him out by pulling my weight to get shit done. Ten minutes later, I took some toast and coffee up to him, carefully handing the coffee over, our fingers brushing.

"Thanks," he said with that ever-present smile. He sipped his coffee but seemed reluctant to take his other hand off the wheel to eat his toast.

So, feeling like a bit of an idiot, I stuck it in front of his mouth. "Bite."

He laughed but chomped into it, and I continued to feed him until it was gone. When he'd taken the last piece, I brushed crumbs off his bottom lip with my thumb which made his eyes flash to mine, and a sexy pink tinged his cheeks.

Well, that was interesting.

"We, uh," he started, now focusing intently toward the land ahead of us. "We'll be arriving in about thirty minutes."

"Then I better go get ready for this hot date," I replied, lightly touching his arm as I went back down below deck.

Showered, dressed, breakfast things washed and dried, I went up the stairs when I heard Foster talking to someone. It was only about the weather or something, but we were obviously mooring, and sure enough, Foster had us backing in to the jetty, parking us like he would a car, in a long row of boats a similar size.

The sail was done already, everything seemed stowed away, and Foster grinned as he stepped with a familiar ease onto the jetty and manoeuvred the mooring line around a post like it was the easiest thing in the world to do. He tied it off in some kind of fancy knot and stepped back on board.

"Just like that, huh?" I asked, amazed at how adept he was. How he knew to do all this stuff...

"Just like that," he replied, still smiling. Then he looked me up and down. "Oh, nice to see you did actually pack some clothes. I was beginning to think you only brought Speedos and underwear."

I looked down at my white shirt, charcoal golf shorts, and grey leather Merrells. "This whole entire outfit cost me a small fortune." I shrugged. "But I can go in my Speedos if you want? I'm sure the locals won't mind."

"If the police don't arrest you for indecent exposure."

"Wearing swimmers isn't illegal."

"It is if they're white and completely see-through when wet."

"Fair point." I laughed. Then I whispered, "Just don't make me wet... while we're in public anyway. I can give you a private viewing later tonight; wet or dry is up to you."

He made a low growly sound. "Your outfit today is fine. Better than fine, in fact."

He was far too easy. "Thanks."

"Have you got everything you need?"

"Yep. I only need my wallet."

"No phone?"

I shook my head. "Nope. Not turning it back on until I absolutely have to."

"Good idea." He stepped off the boat onto the jetty and held out his hand. "You good?"

I took his hand, warm and strong, stepped across, not as smoothly as him, but didn't fall in so I took it as a win. "I am good." I looked up the marina toward the town of Trinity Beach. It was just after seven, so I assumed all the fishing boats were out already, and the recreational boats were getting ready to head out as well. He'd timed it perfectly.

I had organised to pick up a hire car from the marina, so we sorted all that out, and when we'd walked to the car, I went to the driver's side and jingled the keys at him. "Now I'm the captain."

Foster rolled his eyes so hard it looked like it hurt. "Then where to first, captain?"

I snorted out a laugh, but we got into the car and buckled up. "Well, I have open tickets for the SkyRail, the butterfly house, national park entry. Let's do that first. They'll have places to eat, I'm sure. Then when we're done being total tourists for the day, we can hit the market for supplies, and by then we can find somewhere nice for dinner."

"Sounds good. One problem though."

"What's that?"

He was reading a pamphlet the car rental lady had given him. "SkyRail doesn't open till nine. The butterfly place is ten."

"Then a second breakfast on the beach first it is."

He laughed. "Sounds even better."

"But first things first," I said, starting the car and driving out of the car park. "You're going to have to direct me because I don't know where the hell I'm going."

He laughed and pointed ahead. "Take your first left."

He directed me to Trinity Beach where we found a café on the beach. We sat, ordered a huge breakfast, and ate it looking out across the ocean. He smiled at the young waitress, laughed with her when she wrote something down wrong, and told her nothing was a problem.

So typically Foster. Smiling in the sunshine, nothing's an issue, just go with the flow. So very far removed from the corporate life.

I sipped my juice. "You know, sometimes I look at you

and I can see how you would have been ruthless and sharp in finance. And then sometimes, like just now, I can't picture it for anything."

He cocked his head, amused. "How so?"

I took a deep breath, wanting to word this properly. "When I think of finance and mergers and acquisitions, I think grey suits, grey buildings, grey skies. Then I see you here, and it's yellow sunshine, blue skies, white sand, aqua water. It's polar opposites, and it's hard to reconcile."

He smiled as though that summary pleased him, and he put a triangle of fresh pineapple in his mouth. "Because I'm not that man anymore. That's not who I am now. If you'd met me six years ago, you wouldn't have recognised me. I think the only time I ever smiled was when we closed a deal."

I sighed, but he wasn't done.

"And do you think your description of monochrome and dreary settings back home versus sunshine and happiness here is trying to tell you something?"

"Like what?"

He looked me square in the eye. "You're not happy there."

I moved the fork on my empty plate so it sat at twelve and six. "Maybe."

He never said anything back. Maybe he knew I had more to say. Maybe he was using the oldest trick in the corporate book: leave silences and the uncomfortable person will speak first. Maybe I fell for it.

"I'm not happy there," I admitted. It was hardly breaking news. Anyone willing to look could see it. "It wasn't just my idea to take this vacation."

"Your boss saw you were about to crack?"

I shook my head. "My doctor."

That stopped him. He frowned and his eyes narrowed at the table between us. "If you're not happy, that's one thing. But medically..."

"Medically, I was heading for a heart attack or a stroke," I said, admitting more than I wanted to. "High blood pressure, insomnia. Like my mind was stuck in fifth gear, know what I mean?"

He looked at me then, and there was something warm in his eyes. "I know exactly what you mean."

I didn't doubt him, and it was nice, reassuring even, to be able to speak to someone who truly understood what I was going through. Then I cleared my throat and told him what I hadn't ever told anyone else. "I'd had some panic attacks. I didn't know what they were at first. My head went all spacey and my lungs went all tight. I thought I was having a heart attack, or more of a blood pressure thing. I didn't know what the hell it was. Anyway, after a barrage of tests and appointments, my doc told me it was anxiety, and I laughed at her." I shook my head at how stupid this all sounded. "I mean, how could I, Stuart Jenner, have anxiety? I'm at the top of my game. I'm the guy who everyone wants to be. Phone calls, appointments, clients, emails. I'm in such demand, my PA has a PA. It sounds ridiculous, right?"

Foster shook his head slowly. "Not to me. Sounds like you're one phone call, one appointment, one client, one email away from doing a Foster Knight."

"Walking away from everything I've ever known to run a private charter yacht in the tropics?"

He almost smiled. "Well, I don't know about the private charter business, but walking away, yeah."

I met his eyes. "I'm not as brave as you."

He reached over and took my hand on the table. "Yes,

you are. Like you said, you run rings around your competition. That takes balls."

"Yes, but I know that world. I don't know how to not be that guy."

He squeezed my hand. "I could say all it takes is a leap of faith, but it's not really that. It's a case of do or die. Literally. It takes getting to a place in your life when you have no other option but to walk away. One more minute will kill you."

I nodded because he just nailed everything I'd tried to summarise. My voice was barely a whisper. "When do you know? When do you know you've reached that point?"

He gave me a smile that made my heart skip a beat. "Trust me, you'll know." He still held my hand. "You know what you need?"

"What's that?"

"You need a quick walk along the beach after the amount of food we just ate. Then you need a day sightseeing and hiking and a relaxing dinner overlooking the ocean. A few beers, maybe something more."

He had a glint in his eye that matched his smile. It made me smile in return. "Will there be tequila straight from the bottle? Lick, sip, suck happens to be my new favourite game."

He chuckled. "Not sure the tequila's necessary, but sure."

I drained the rest of my juice, glad the seriousness from before was gone. "I'm just glad we didn't decide to play a game with martinis. Not sure where the olives would go."

He laughed and stood up, keeping hold of my hand. "Come on, let's walk off some of those ridiculous calories we just inhaled." We waved goodbye to the waitress and took the steps down to the sand and headed up away from where the tourists and locals were now milling around the town.

"I can't tell you the last time I ate eggs and bacon and toast."

"It'll do you the world of good," Foster said. "How about we make today the day Stuart does a whole lotta stuff he wouldn't normally do. I want to see you smile all day long, and by the time we get back on board tonight, I want you to tell me you had the best day ever."

I stopped walking. "Well, if you give me a happy ending when we get back on the boat, I'm sure it will be."

He laughed and pushed my shoulder. "That's not what I meant."

"But?"

He slid his arm around my shoulder and we started to walk down to the water, heading up the beach. "But that depends. You said you liked to be fucked *into* the mattress. Was that a metaphorical thing, or are we talking literal, *inside the mattress*, because that could get weird."

Now it was me who laughed. "I'm pretty sure I'd be happy with either, to be honest."

He smiled serenely at the water. "This is nice, yeah? Walking up the beach, my arm around your shoulder?"

I nodded. "Yeah, it is. And if we're ticking things off the 'Stuart's never done' list, then we can add this."

"Never?"

I shook my head. "Never had the time."

He gave me a squeeze, then slung his arm around my neck like it was the most natural thing in the world. "Well, I'm glad I'm your first."

The thing was, I had a feeling Foster might be my first for a lot of things. "Me too."

THE SKYRAIL WAS AWESOME, although I was hoping we would have a carriage to ourselves, but an older, grey-haired couple were bundled in after us, the doors closing the four of us in. They sat facing us, with kind enough smiles, but I could see it on their faces they didn't know what to make of us. Two guys sitting close enough to touch from knee to shoulder. "Nice day for it," Foster prompted.

"Most certainly is," the lady replied.

And then there was an awkward silence, and when we got to the first of two stops and it was pretty clear they weren't getting out, Foster grabbed my hand and, laughing, we ducked out of the carriage.

There were two stops along the SkyRail that allowed people to get out and explore the rainforest, and given the guide at the base explained the second one was more popular, I was glad we got out at the first.

We had the trail to ourselves.

The air was thick and humid, dank with rainforest undergrowth, loud with birds. Everything was every possible shade of green, and filtered sunlight covered the path. It was kinda perfect.

Foster grinned as he faced me. He threaded our fingers and led the way along the path.

"I'm pretty sure this is how some of *Australia's Most Wanted* episodes start," I joked as he pulled me deeper along the forest path. "Or 'Little Red Riding Hood.' I should have worn my red shirt."

His laughter rang out in the trees, birds replying overhead. Then he stopped and pulled me against him and said, "My, what beautiful lips you have."

"All the better to suck dick with," I replied, grinning.

He chuckled. "I was going for 'all the better to kiss you with' but that works." Then he kissed me, chaste and sweet, sending a thrill through my body. My heart thumped and my blood felt electric, but he pulled away all too quick and grinned as he led me further down the path.

The forest was beautiful; the hike was invigorating. It was tiring, using muscles I hadn't used in ages, but I felt so good. We laughed, we talked, we took our time, never rushing. It never felt strange that we held hands or that we stole kisses every now and then. We were acting like boyfriends, and that should've been weird, but it wasn't. It felt so natural, so right. And if holiday flings allowed us to break from our realities and be something else, then why question it?

Foster certainly wasn't questioning it when he was the one to grab my hand or slip his arm around my waist. The way he smiled, so free, without stress weighing him down, without a care in the world—it damn near took my breath away.

I took photos of him in front of ferns so big, his outstretched arms couldn't measure. In front of trees that made him look tiny, in front of views that simply didn't compare to the man in focus. "Selfie time," he cried when we were back at the SkyRail. The view behind us was pretty incredible, but seriously, when I saw that photo of our heads together, our huge smiles, I almost didn't recognise myself.

I looked happy.

When we reached the bottom, we grabbed some lunch from the café and sat under the trees outside to eat it. He was so laid back, like we had all the time in the world, and I realised something then, watching him, was that his peacefulness didn't come from the lack of high-stress, fast-paced corporate life.

It came from within. Like he'd found Zen or something.

I couldn't even be too jealous because I admired him too much.

"Stuart? You in there?" Foster was looking at me weirdly.

He'd obviously been trying to get my attention. "Oh, sorry. Just thinking. What did you say?"

"I asked if you were ready to go?"

I looked down at my empty sandwich wrapper, which I didn't strictly remember eating, finished my water, and nodded. "Yep."

He jumped to his feet and held out his hand, quickly pulling me up. We threw our rubbish into the recycling bin, and about thirty minutes later, we arrived at the Butterfly Sanctuary. Now truth be told, I didn't think it'd be my thing, and I only agreed to go because the travel agent talked me into it, but it fit in with my 'things Stuart has never done' theme for the day.

We walked into the butterfly house, and all of a sudden it was like we'd walked into a fairy tale; the dome had a magical feel, with greenery, and in no time, we were surrounded by butterflies. And not just your average garden variety, but huge, bright-coloured ones. Some were blue, some were green, some were the size of birds.

The guide told us about the fight to save the species and how the blue butterfly, the big gorgeous one, had been saved by some butterfly doctor from Tasmania. We got to hold out halved oranges in our hands, and they flittered down to us.

They were so delicate, so remarkable. I'd never even considered butterflies before, but I was utterly blown away. And from the look on Foster's face, he felt the same.

When the tour was over, we took a guided safari ride into the park, through rivers, through the forest, and sitting in the open-top truck, Foster took my hand and held it on his thigh. "This is kind of special, isn't it?"

My eyes shot to his, wondering what he was talking about. Us? Getting to spend the day with each other, pretending to be boyfriends? Is that what he meant?

He laughed and waved his free hand in an arc. "This whole place. Those butterflies were just... Wow."

"It was pretty amazing," I replied, not letting my disappointment show. Fuck. Why was I even disappointed? Surely he couldn't have been talking about me. Or us. There was no us. I was his paying client; I was literally paying him to spend the day with me...

But then he threaded our fingers and nudged his shoulder to mine. "The whole day has been amazing. The SkyRail, the butterflies. This, here, with you. All of it. Thank you."

I pretended I wasn't blushing, that his words didn't make my heart thump. "What are you thanking me for?"

"For inviting me. For asking me to spend the day with you." He squeezed my hand. "I haven't had this much fun in ages."

"I thought cruising around the tropical islands was your idea of fun," I said, nudging his shoulder this time.

"It is. But there's fun to be had on land too. I'm so used to being on water, I didn't think I'd be able to walk properly."

I leaned in close and whispered, "Is that what all the boys say?"

He chuckled and tightened his grip. "Dunno. You'll have to let me know tomorrow."

Holy shit. Okay, so we were both on the same page

about what we wanted tonight. "That's good to know. I'll keep you posted."

He laughed and the guide stopped talking to stare at us. I felt like a school kid busted for talking in class, and Foster waited until the guide started talking again before he leaned into me to muffle his laughter.

He smiled all the way back into Palm Cove, and I guess I did too. I'd promised him a fancy dinner, and given we were wearing shorts and shirts, the fanciest our dress code allowed for was a waterfront bar and grill. We were given a table for two on the deck and ordered a beer each while we went over the menu and wine list.

It was getting late. We'd literally been out the entire day, and the view of palm trees over the water as the sun set was truly spectacular.

The company was even better.

Foster told me how, when he started his business, people were sceptical of the city slicker lasting more than a week. But he proved them wrong, won them over with his charm and his ability to listen and learn.

"And I'm pretty sure that smile helped too," I added.

He chuckled. "Maybe. But they soon figured out I was here to stay and that I ran a good business. I'm not here to make millions; I'm here for the lifestyle. I care for the environment, and that won me some votes."

"So, are you a local yet?" I asked.

He snorted. "Jim Scott, the guy who owns the company I contract for, he's been here for forty years, and he's only just got his membership to local status."

I laughed at that. "Exclusive club, huh?"

We ordered a dinner of swordfish, Wagyu ribeye medallions, and salad. Foster chose the white wine for us, and we ate by candlelight and the overhead fairy lights. It was, hands down, the most romantic dinner of my life.

Unplanned, unscripted, and completely unbelievable.

I wanted it to last forever. I wanted this fantasy holiday to be my real life, and now, along with going back to a job I didn't want, I'd be going back to being alone.

To not having this. To missing this. I never knew I wanted this, until now. I thought all I wanted in life was a casual hook-up, no strings attached. It was all I ever had time for, and it had worked well for me until now.

Until Foster.

Until I knew what I was missing.

"What would you do," Foster started, "if you left your life in Brisbane and moved here?"

"Here?"

He shrugged. "Well, anywhere. If you were no longer in mergers and acquisitions, what would Stuart Jenner do? Stay in Brisbane? Move?"

I sipped my wine while I thought of my answer. "I don't know. I... I've never thought about it before. I mean, I've thought about it—God, I've dreamed of it—but what can I do? I don't know how to do anything else."

He stared at me, unblinking. "Yes, you do."

"What? Model for Speedo?"

He laughed. "Hell yes. They'd be fools not to take you."

I rolled my eyes and took another sip of wine.

"You read the stock market," he said seriously. "You know finance. You predict trends that can shape the economy."

"Yes, but you said if I was no longer in finance."

"So why can't you move into financial advising?"

"Because I'm not qualified."

"You'd get qualified in no time. Hell, you could work the stock market for a living."

"I thought I was supposed to be finding something less stressful."

He laughed again. "Low-key, long-term. You know how it works for an individual investor."

"Why didn't you do that?" I countered. "If it's that easy."

"I dabble in the stock market, now and then. But I have my dream job."

I swirled the wine around the glass, not taking my eyes off his. "You make it sound so easy."

"It is. You'll see. One day you'll reach that point, that tipping point, where if you don't walk away, you'll feel like you're dying. I hope you don't. I really hope you don't. But..."

"But I'm already close?"

He stared at me for a long moment. "I don't know you that well, Stuart. But I reckon I know you well enough to know you want to get out."

I laughed, a quiet, bitter sound. "See? That's where you're wrong."

"You don't want to quit?"

I shook my head. "No, not that. You said you don't know me that well. Foster, you're the only person on the planet that knows me at all."

CHAPTER TWELVE

FOSTER

DINNER WAS PERFECT, then I had to go ruin it with talking about his job, about him leaving and going back to a job, to a life, he hates. The light in his eyes snuffed out as soon as I mentioned it, and I regretted it the second those stupid words left my mouth.

I needed to make it up to him. I needed to distract him and lift his mood again. We'd had the best day. The very best, if I was being honest, and I didn't want it to end on a sour note.

I didn't want it to end at all.

Then he told me I was the only person to know the real him. Jesus, I'd known him for a handful of days. We'd discussed personal subjects. He'd admitted some things his colleagues could never know about his dreams and his health. I got the feeling he was being himself with me, and I hated that he was guarded in his real life.

"Thank you," I said.

"What for?" His tone was disbelief, frustration, resignation.

"For today. For inviting me to join you. I've had one of

the best days I've had in ages. And thank you for showing me who you really are."

He almost flinched, his eyes narrowing. "You make it sound like that's a bad thing."

I shook my head slowly, not taking my eyes from his. "Oh no, Stuart. Just the opposite. It's a very good thing."

He looked down at the table, and a dozen emotions crossed his face in the flickering of the fairy lights. "I have no reason to be anything but myself with you."

I reached over and took his hand. "That's what I'm thanking you for. It's a privilege to witness."

He shook his head like he could physically rebuff my compliment. I assumed professional accolades were par for the course with him, but anything remotely personal was out of bounds. "Don't we need to hit the supermarket? I need to have the car back by nine, so..."

"So, let's go," I said, standing up.

He insisted on paying "because I asked you out, Foster, it's only right" so I let him, and I was kind of glad we weren't going straight back to the marina. Granted, grocery shopping was no romantic prelude to... well, anything, but it gave me a chance to make him smile before we went back to the yacht.

I got better than a smile, though. As soon as we walked through the doors, there was a huge box of lemons and limes, and Stuart laughed as he bagged about twenty.

"I don't think we'll need that many," I tried to reason.

"There will be lots of lick, sip, sucking."

I cringed. "I have serious concerns for my liver."

He laughed and leaned in close. "I have serious concerns for my arse because I know what you're packing. So I'll call us even."

I laughed louder than was probably polite in a grocery

store, and just like that, we were back to smiles, gentle touches, and heated glances. The darker topics of reality were left behind for now.

We picked fresh fruits and veggies, cuts of meat, and seafood. "Want some oysters?" I asked, looking in the deli fridge.

Stuart's nostrils flared and he made a face. "Not a fan. But by all means, you can. I've heard they're... beneficial."

I snorted. "Nah. What about some fresh prawns?"

"Yeah, sounds good."

When we were about done, I nodded my head toward the far aisle. "Personals aisle. Should we check it out?" I started walking and he did follow, but when I'd stopped at the condoms and lube section, I gave him a raised eyebrow. "Any particular favourites?"

He shrugged. "I actually packed a twelve-pack. I had my bag packed before Mr Arsehole decided he'd rather not join me. I never took them out."

"Oh." I picked up a tube of lube.

"And lube. I'm always prepared."

I snorted. "How many were in the pack you said you have?" I asked.

"Twelve."

"Hmm." I pretended to consider this. "And how many days do we have? Will that be enough?"

He laughed. "Don't tease me like that. Or I'll hold you to it."

"We do dock again in another three days, so we should be right until then," I joked. I picked up a sensual massage oil and threw it in the basket. "If you're lucky, I'll let you give me a full body massage."

He snorted. "Gee, thanks. But just so you know, I

wouldn't be terribly opposed. Actually, the more I think about it..." He got a faraway look in his eyes, then readjusted his crotch. "Yeah, maybe I shouldn't be thinking about it."

I ran a hand down his back and over his arse, giving it a squeeze. "Last stop is the liquor department. Then we're back on the yacht where you can think about it all you like."

We got to the checkout, and he looked at the basket. "I'm paying for this," I stated, knowing what he was about to say. "It's part of your tour." There really wasn't a great deal in it, to be honest, and he'd already paid for dinner...

"I'll get the alcohol," he said, walking through the registers, where I couldn't go with my unpaid goods. "That's only fair."

I sighed. I couldn't argue; he was already gone, and the checkout guy was smiling at me expectantly. I loaded our things through, and by the time I was done, he came back out with a grin a mile wide, carrying a carton of Corona with a bottle of Alquimia Reserva de Don Adolfo Extra Añejo tequila on top. "Was that completely necessary?" I asked as we walked out toward the car.

"Completely."

I couldn't even chastise him for spending so much money; it was supposed to be a fully catered charter after all, but his grin was so beautiful, I couldn't do anything but smile in return. I guess the rules changed about a lot of things when it was just the two of us.

I guess a lot of things changed.

We handed over the keys to the car and carried our supplies down the jetty to the yacht. There were a few people about, a few lights on here and there, but mostly we were alone. Stuart slid the carton of beer onto the dining table. "So, do we stay docked here for the night, or do we make a start for our next stop?"

"We stay here. Why? Did you not want to?"

"Oh, no, I don't mind either way. I just wondered, if the yacht gets rocking too much, people will notice." He grinned. "I'd hate to be interrupted when you find your rhythm. If you know what I mean..."

I smiled as I put the groceries away. "Oh, I know what you mean. But this yacht has pretty good water displacement ratios. It won't rock too much."

He put the bottle of tequila on the counter beside me and kissed the back of my neck, his body pressing against me. "Know that from experience?"

"Not personally," I replied. I didn't mean to sound so breathless, so desperate. I let my head fall back onto his shoulder and he kissed along my neck. "Other people..."

He paused at my ear, his breath warm. His tongue made my knees weak. "You've never fucked anyone on your own yacht?"

"No." I gripped the counter to stop myself from turning around. "Always kept it on shore, if you know what I mean."

"Isn't this your house?" he asked, pushing me harder against the cabinets, his cock pressing hot and hard against my arse.

I could barely manage a one-word response. "Yes."

He grinded against me, slow and hard. "So I'll be the first guy you fuck here?"

"Yes."

He clearly liked that because he melted against me, and his cock pulsed. "My bed," he murmured, "or yours?"

"Mine, yours. I don't fucking care." I tried to turn, but he kept me pinned. I could feel his smile as he kissed down my neck.

"Do you want a shot of tequila? Want to lick the salt off my body?"

I shook my head. "No. I don't need it." I turned around then and he let me. His eyes were dark and his smile predatory. I could see why he had a list of friends with benefits. If he looked at anyone the way he was looking at me right now... "I don't need the courage and I don't want the inhibitor," I said. I fisted his shirt and pulled him close, our hips aligning, my erection against his. "I want to feel everything."

His nostrils flared and he crushed his mouth to mine in a consuming kiss. Hot and passionate, his hand went to my face, my hair, holding my neck, and he pushed me back against the sink. When he finally drew back, he was breathless and his lips were wet and plump. "Lock the door, captain. Your cabin boy needs a really good fucking."

Jesus.

I almost came right then. I had to give myself a squeeze to stem the pleasure. He grinned like a smug arsehole and walked into his room, peeling his shirt off as he went.

Right then.

Move, Foster.

I jolted into action, closing the cabin door and locking it. I flipped the lights off as I went and found him wearing nothing but underwear. He smirked as he slid them down, watching my eyes as he stepped out of them. He went to his suitcase, pulled out a box of condoms and a bottle of lube, and threw them on the bed. He straightened out a towel in the middle of the mattress and gave me a filthy smirk as he knelt over it.

His cock jutted out, rock hard. He gave himself a slow pump. "I've been waiting for this," he said.

"No pressure then," I said.

"Oh, I know you'll make this good for me, Foster." He all but purred the words. He leant over, showing me the most delicious looking arse I'd ever seen, putting on a show as he took the lube and slicked his finger. Then he straightened up, reached around, and rubbed his finger over his hole.

"Oh fuck," I breathed.

"Do you want to watch me fuck myself?" he asked. "Or would you like to actually get naked at some point and do it for me?"

He said he was in control in the bedroom, and I shouldn't have doubted him. I was still standing there watching him and he groaned as he slipped a finger inside. It was a guttural sound, a mix of pleasure and impatience. I took the hint and stripped off, giving my cock a hard squeeze. At this point, I'd come before I was even inside him.

Kneeling on the bed behind him, I ran my hand over his lower back, over his arse cheek, spreading him so his finger had better access. "You're so fucking hot," I mumbled. "Jesus, Stuart, I could come just from watching you."

He chuckled, gruff and desperate. "Not tonight. Tonight, I need you in me. Now, Foster. I'm not kidding."

I took a foil wrapper and ripped it open, rolling the condom down my cock and giving my balls a tug. This was going to be embarrassing.

Fuck! Get a grip, Foster.

I lubed myself up, then my fingers. "Take your hand away," I said.

Stuart did as I asked but arched his back, sticking his arse out and looking upward. "You better hurry up and get something inside—"

I gripped his shoulder and thrust one finger inside him, making his words die in his throat. "That's just one finger."

"Fuck yes," he groaned.

I pumped my finger in and out a few times, slow and deep. He was hot and tight and so fucking receptive. He made a deep whining sound that became the word "more."

So I added a second finger and he arched again, pushing down on my hand. *Fuck. He was loving it.* "You like that?" I asked.

"Want more. Need more," he moaned, his head lolling back like he was lost to the sensation. "Your cock. Please."

Oh, sweet Lord have mercy.

I pulled my fingers out and he whimpered, so I shuffled in behind him, the backs of his thighs flush against me. Using one hand to grip his hip and the other to guide me inside him, I pushed in.

He took me, all of me, so perfectly, so completely.

He groaned as every inch of me filled him. I gripped his hips and paused when I was buried as deep as I could go, to steady myself, to breathe.

"Fuck, Stuart," I whispered against his spine. He was basically straddling me, sitting on my cock, reverse cowboy, his back against my front. "You good?"

He moaned, long and loud, his head against my neck. He was panting and whining. "Move in me."

I rolled my hips and he jerked up, crying out. He gripped my hair, and at first, I thought I'd hurt him, but he rocked on me, trying to fuck. "Do that again," he pleaded. "More."

So I did, and he reacted the same way. I did it over and over and he jerked himself and I was hurtling toward my orgasm; faster, more intense, more powerful than any I'd ever felt. I couldn't stop it, not even if I wanted to.

"Stuart, I'm gonna come," I ground out.

He threw his head back and a strangled cry ripped from his chest as he came, stripes of come shooting onto the towel. He stiffened, squeezing my cock, and I drove up into him as my orgasm obliterated my senses. Sight and sound fell away as bliss imploded within me. I cried out as I filled the condom, and he grunted in time with the pulsing inside him.

He fell back against me, his hands reaching up to my head. I never wanted to leave his body. I never wanted this, right here, to end. Not this feeling, not this moment.

I put an arm around his chest and gently lowered him to the mattress, pressing my weight onto his back. I was still inside him, and he sighed. I ran my hands along his arms, and when I got to his hands, he quickly threaded our fingers. "I never want to move," I whispered, kissing the nape of his neck.

His voice was languid and husky. "Stay inside me and I'll come again."

I chuckled. "Is that so?"

"Yes." He answered so fast and sure, like it was the God's honest truth.

"I need to take the condom off," I mumbled but not attempting to move.

"Put another one on and get back inside me."

I chuckled again and slowly pulled my hips back until I slipped free of him. I discarded the condom, and when I looked back at Stuart, he was still on his front, holding up another foil wrapper. "I wasn't kidding."

I blinked and looked down at my spent dick. Okay, it was still half-hard, but I wasn't sure... "After *that* orgasm, I'm not sure I can."

He smirked. "Oh, believe me, you have another one in you tonight."

I snorted and knelt on the bed, crawling back up his body. I kissed his arse cheek, the base of his spine, then up to his neck. "How do you know?"

He hummed, enjoying my soft kisses. "I just know."

"Sex with you is fucking good," I allowed.

"Just good?"

"Mind-blowing. Best I've ever had."

He began to turn around "The best—"

I pushed his shoulder back onto the bed, held him down, and whispered in his ear. "Don't let it go to your head."

He smiled into the mattress and lifted his hips against my dick. "I can feel your cock getting harder already. Now suit up and get the fuck back inside me."

"You like being bossy in the bedroom?" I asked. "Or do you want me to show you who's really in charge?"

He turned his head and his eyes were molten brown. "Do you think you're good enough to fuck me into the mattress?" Then he stretched out, shoving a pillow under his head, and spread his legs and lifted his arse just so.

He smiled into the pillow when he heard me tear into the foil wrapper. He pulled his head back and moaned when I sunk inside him again. And so help me God, he wasn't wrong. All he needed was a cock buried inside him to make him come, and he really loved getting pounded into the mattress.

And after I'd wrung a second orgasm out of him, followed directly by my own, we collapsed in a sweaty, panting mess. I had every intention of getting up and going to my own bed. I had no idea if Stuart was opposed to having a guy sleep in his bed, and I was about to ask him when he pulled me against him, burrowed himself into my chest, and was out like a light. I sighed and kissed his forehead, feeling happier and more content than I could ever remember, and fell into a deep and blissful sleep.

CHAPTER THIRTEEN

STUART

I WOKE UP SMILING. I hadn't done that in years. I ached in all the right places and I felt relaxed and limber. I stretched and rolled over to find my bed empty, but there was the smell of something amazing coming from the kitchen. Or galley. Whatever.

I slipped into the shower, scrubbed myself clean of lube and dried come, brushed my teeth, shaved, and pulled on my swimmers.

When I opened my bedroom door, Foster looked me up and down, saw I was wearing my Speedos and nothing else, and laughed. "You are merciless."

"Good morning to you too."

"I was hoping to have this cooked before you woke up."

"It smells good."

"Omelette with mushrooms, capsicum, bacon with toast. How are you feeling?" He slid a coffee across the counter to me.

"I feel good." I sipped the coffee and hummed. "How did you sleep?"

"Like the dead." He slid the omelette onto the toast on each plate and we sat at the table. "How about you?"

"Like I was thoroughly had."

He smiled as he chewed. "Yes, you were."

I ate a few mouthfuls. "This is really good."

He nodded slowly. "Are you... sore at all?"

"In a good way. Are you... okay? With... what we did?"

He made a surprised sound and blushed as he studied his plate. "Uh, very." He looked at me and swallowed hard. "Very okay."

"So there'll be more *thoroughly having* later, then?"

Foster sipped his coffee and smiled at me over the cup. "When you're up for it."

I looked at my non-existent watch. "Lunchtime good for you?"

He laughed, and after a happy moment of silence passed between us, he changed the subject. "So, I thought we'd head out to Ellis Beach today, then be back out along the reef tonight. How does that sound?"

I nodded. "Sounds great."

"You wanna help me sail out of the harbour?"

"Hell yes."

He laughed. "Well then, finish your breakfast and we'll up anchor."

Thirty minutes later, we were heading up the coast past Palm Cove, where we'd had dinner, and on our way to Ellis Beach on Double Island. It was stunningly beautiful; white sand, palm trees, rainforest greenery, and water so blue it didn't even look real.

It was also a tourist hotspot, with a few dozen charter boats in these parts on any given day, and while I would have loved to have one of the beaches to ourselves, it just wasn't possible.

Foster didn't ask me to pull the mainsail down, so I asked him, "Are we stopping here for a swim?"

"Well, you can," he replied. "But those nets off the beach are for Irukandji jellyfish. And they do get the odd three-metre saltwater crocodile swim over from the mainland."

I blinked at him. "So, that's a no."

He grinned. "On the bright side, that means there's less likely to be sharks."

I could feel the blood drain from my face. "Why did you have to mention sharks? I've been in there, where there could be sharks? Jesus Christ."

He cracked up laughing. "Do you honestly think I'd let you swim in waters known for shark sightings? You've been swimming mostly on the reef shallows, which are actually pretty safe. Only reef sharks and the occasional white tip, which aren't to be confused with the great white. Though there is the occasional tiger shark or hammerhead, but they're rare. And we all get warnings if there's been a sighting, so I would have known."

I blinked again. "I'm never swimming in the ocean again."

Foster laughed some more. "Yes you will. You'll be fine. I promise. In six years, I've never even seen anything but small reef sharks, and they're afraid of humans. Anyway, the more dangerous sharks prefer the deeper, colder waters in the southern states. We'll be fine."

"I don't want to see any kind of shark."

His grin widened. "It's the ones you can't see you need to worry about."

I thumped his arm. "You're not helping."

He just laughed and nudged me with his elbow. "I'm just kidding. I promise."

"Well, I'm still not swimming again."

He took his hand off the wheel and cupped my face. "Yes you will. I'm sorry, I was just joking around. I didn't mean to scare you." He pulled me in for a kiss, which was new for us. It was unprompted, early in the day, and there was no tequila or lemons involved. "And anyway, if you don't get in the water, how will I lick the salt off your skin?"

He made me smile, despite me trying not to. "I can think of something else you can lick if you want something salty."

He rolled his eyes and laughed, and he began to pull away but then stole another quick kiss before going back to the wheel. "We can head straight out to the reef, but I want you to plot our course."

"What?"

"On the GPS. I want to head northeast, to the top of Oyster Reef and the bottom of Michaelmas." He took in my blank stare, then shooed me toward the digital screens. "And I want you to tell me how to get there."

I'd watched him do this, and I'd listened as he'd shown me, but I'd never done it by myself. So I took a deep breath and found the place he was talking about, punched it in, and relayed the coordinates. I had no doubts he could find his way there without the GPS; he was doing this for my benefit, not his.

"Wind direction?"

I searched the multi-purpose screen for the correct wind information. "Um, southerly."

"Speed?"

"Five knots."

"Okay, what is my point of sail?"

Shit. I tried to remember what he'd said... "Um, broad reach?"

He smiled, so I knew I was right. "What's my VMG?"

"Your what?"

"Velocity Made Good. The speed and the direction to our destination."

Fuck. "Yeah, about that. When you were explaining that part, I tuned out when you started with physics and trigonometry."

He threw his head back and laughed. "It's the boat speed. On the screen, bottom corner."

"Why didn't you just say that?" I shot back at him. "Four point six."

He flashed me a handsome grin. "See? You'll make a sailor yet."

"Oh, please. The only sailor I'd make is in Fleet Week."

He laughed and I sat on the bench seat beside him. He was standing at the wheel, and as much as I loved sunbaking and snorkelling, I loved this part the most. The sea breeze in my hair, the glide of the yacht in the water, the sound of the wind in the sail. I loved the speed of it, the sleekness, the hydrodynamics of it all. It was an adrenaline rush, and with the wind in our favour, we made the reef in no time at all.

Foster had me bring in the mainsail and hoist the smaller headsail. Our pace slowed dramatically as he navigated around the top of Oyster Reef to sneak in under Michaelmas. The water was shallower and the prettiest colour turquoise I'd ever seen. I could see the sandy bottom where we dropped anchor and the fish that swam around the coral just a few metres away.

"Holy shit, that's incredible," I said, looking off the back of the yacht.

"Still don't want to get in?" Foster asked.

"Maybe. If you come with me." I didn't want to get in

the water without him in case I had another freak-out, but now I could play it off for shark-related reasons.

He rolled his eyes. "You might twist my arm." He lowered the ladder but then went about doing something with the screens. I sat on the back and dangled my feet in the water. The water was warm but still a damn sight cooler than sitting in the scorching sun for twenty minutes.

When I'd had enough, I ducked into the cockpit and found the sunscreen, then went in search of Foster. I got as far as the galley when he came out of his room wearing his boardies, which meant we were swimming.

My grin was immediate and I held up the sunscreen like a trophy. "Just in time."

I did his back first, then his chest, down his abs, while I gave him fuck-me eyes and let my tongue peek out. "I was thinking we could have a swim now," I said, being all flirty and shit. "Then maybe lie in the sun a bit to dry off, make out a bit, then have some lunch, then you can fuck me again, then maybe another swim before dinner. Then we can do round two where you bury yourself inside me for hours. How does that sound?" I handed him the sunscreen and cocked an eyebrow.

He snatched the bottle, spun me around, and pressed me against the table, his cock against my arse as he whispered hot and gruff in my ear, "You won't win this game against me."

He squirted cold sunscreen onto my skin, rubbed my shoulders, my back, pushing me so I was bent over the table, pinned by his hips, his hard length rubbing my arse crack. I wanted to just pull down my Speedos and beg him to fill me, but by the time I could formulate thoughts into words, he was gone. "Your back's done. I'll get our towels."

I stood up, panting and a little light-headed, and

extremely turned on. My cock barely fit in my swimmers, tenting the fabric, and when he walked back out of his room, he looked at my face, my crotch, back to my face, and he smiled. "Oh my, that's a really big problem you have there." Then he threw a clean towel at me and laughed as he went up the stairs. "Last one in's a rotten egg!"

"I hate you," I called and his laughter was his only reply.

I followed him up just in time to see him dive in, and he grinned up at me from the water. "Get your beautiful arse in the water," he said.

I dropped the towel and jumped in. I was hoping the water might lessen my hard-on, but it was warm enough to make it feel good. And of course, Foster swam straight over to me, and with his body almost flush with mine, he kissed me. "Was I a bit mean to you before?"

"Yes. It was cruel to tease me like that."

He laughed. "I'll make it up to you later."

"You better."

"Let me see if I've got this in order," he said with a grin. "Sunbake, making out, lunch, swim, sex, dinner, more sex."

"Correct. Though I hope you're open to improvisation."

"Why's that?"

"Because I might need to shuffle the sex to before lunch, then making out after."

He grinned. "I can adapt."

And adapt he did. We started out lazing on the deck, sprawled in the sun to dry off, which led to touching, to making out, to me rolling on top of Foster and grinding down on him. I was well past caring if passing boats saw us; I had more pressing needs.

So he took me down to my room, laid me on the bed,

and I was so turned on, I came as soon as he was fully seated inside me.

The rest of the day went as I'd planned. Feeding each other fruit, licking juices off chins, off lips, snoozing in each other's arms, more swimming, cooking dinner, and more sex, and I fell asleep in his arms in my crumpled-up bed, exhausted, sated. And for the first time in a long time, happy.

THE TWO DAYS that followed were much the same. We sailed around Hastings Reef, up to Tongue Reef, then went east up to below Opal Reef, and when we weren't sailing, we were swimming, snorkelling, lazing in the sun, making out, and having incredible, *incredible* sex.

The weather was perfect. Blue skies, still waters that varied in shades of blue: cerulean, turquoise, aqua, and teal. The sun was scorching, the food was incredible, tequila shots were fun, and Foster was... well, he was a remarkable man.

We talked about everything from finance and the world economy to the environment, to childhood aspirations of what we'd wanted to be when we grew up. We shared our histories of first kisses, of first times, bad haircuts, and happiest childhood memories.

We were comfortable around each other, *with* each other. If I'd been isolated with anyone else, I'd have probably gone mad confined to a fourteen-metre yacht. But we moved around the space with ease, taking time out when we needed, taking touches and stealing kisses too.

He taught me how to tie different knots, how to make

that salad dressing, which hand signals meant what when we were snorkelling, and he schooled me in bed.

"Do you think if we sailed away, anyone would notice?" I asked. We were lazing on the deck soaking up sunshine. He was wearing his boardies with no shirt, I wore my Speedos, and I had my head on his hip and he had his fingers in my hair, gently pulling at strands in a relaxing, never-want-to-move kind of way.

Foster chuckled. "Uh, yeah. Pretty sure they would. You're booked in at Turtle Cove tomorrow, aren't you?"

"Turtle Cove?"

"Yeah, the gay resort," he reminded me. "Pretty sure that's what it says in my log. I'm to drop you there for an overnight stay."

"Ugh. I forgot." I sighed. Turtle Cove resort...

He was right, though. I had a night's stay at the resort booked. It was recommended by the travel agency to break up the second half of the sailing trip. It allowed us to stand on solid ground for a while and gave Foster a chance to restock food and water supplies. It also happened to be an exclusive gay resort where clothing was optional. I'd originally booked it because I was supposed to be there with Jason, and the plan had been to maybe find another couple to join us.

But that certainly wasn't going to happen now, and now there was Foster and me...

I didn't want to be at a gay resort by myself. I certainly didn't want to hook up with some random guy, considering I had more than enough sex with Foster to keep me happy.

I sighed, not sure how I felt about any of it, not that there was much I could do about it. It was booked and paid for, and Foster would need me off the yacht so he could do what he needed to do. And it was just one night.

"What's the matter?" Foster asked.

I turned my head, pressing my ear against the soft skin of his belly, so I could look him in the eyes. "Do I have to go?"

"You don't want to do a bit of shopping? Do something different?"

I looked at him as though he'd lost his damn mind. "That'd be a no."

"I've organised to get a grocery delivery, and I usually give the yacht a clean."

"Do you want me to go?"

He tried not to smile. "I have some things I need to do. Some work things. Not very fun things I'd rather not talk about with you."

"Why?"

He answered my question with a question. "Isn't it all paid for anyway?"

"Yeah. So what?"

"So then go."

It sounded like he wanted me off the boat. I turned back to look at the sky. "I can take a hint."

"I hear the food's good. There's a cocktail bar and a swim-up bar in the pool."

"And a lot of guys looking for a single guy like me to take advantage of. Remind me to pack the tequila. Sounds like I'll need it."

His fingers stilled in my hair, but I didn't give him the satisfaction of looking at him. "I'm going for a swim. Wanna join me?" I got up and walked to the back of the yacht and dived in. A few minutes later I heard a splash behind me, and soon he slid his arm around my waist. He didn't say anything. He just pressed his lips to the back of my neck, behind my ear. Then his kisses became bites and his hold on me became tickles, and in no time we were laughing and splashing each other, then trying to dunk each other, then holding each other, wrapping limbs around each other, and kissing and getting desperate. Then we were soon back on the boat and on my bed.

He really was very good at distraction.

I was face down on the mattress, having not moved a muscle afterwards, and I'd almost dozed off when he goosed my arse, making me jump. "What?" I grumbled, opening my eyes.

He planted a kiss on my shoulder. "I asked if you wanted grilled chicken or pasta for dinner."

"Mmm, grilled chicken and pasta."

He snorted. "Of course you do."

"I'll get up in a sec and help you make it," I mumbled.

"Stay right where you are." Then he snorted. "I doubt you could move even if you wanted to."

I chuckled, a husky, sleepy sound. "I think you took the phrase 'fuck me into the mattress' too literal."

He pulled on his shorts and I opened my eyes enough to see him grin. "You're welcome."

"Hmm."

It took me about twenty minutes before I could muster the strength, or the will, to move. I ached in all the right places and had that fluid and limber feeling in my bones that only phenomenal sex could give. Then after dinner, with a belly full of carbs, I could barely keep my eyes open.

He pulled me into his room—which was new because we'd always slept in mine—put me on his bed, crawled in behind me, and pulled me into his arms.

I didn't give tomorrow another thought. I was too wrapped up in him, his warmth, his strength, his smell, his lips against my forehead. I was asleep in no time.

WE ARRIVED at the private jetty above Port Douglas before lunch. The resort was accessible from the road, but most guests arrived from Port Douglas by shuttle boat—it gave the guests the feeling of exclusivity and luxury, apparently.

It also meant Foster could dock right there, and all I had to do was walk off the yacht, down the jetty, along the path through sprawling gardens to the resort.

It was grand and elite, and I could see it was worth every penny it cost me. I'd been kind of quiet in the morning, helping Foster bring the yacht into the mainland. So we were busy, but I was also a little pissed that he wanted to get rid of me for the day. Okay, so maybe pissed wasn't the right word. I was disappointed, and his rejection stung like a bitch.

So maybe a day on solid ground would do me good. I could talk to someone different in a space bigger than just a few metres across. It wasn't like I had any claim on Foster. We weren't anything to each other, more than skipper and client.

Maybe it was the reminder that stung the most.

I dumped my bag at the reception desk. The young guy behind the desk was blond, blue-eyed, with tanned skin, utterly pretty pink lips, and looked like he'd walked off the swim team. I was pretty sure he was chosen for reception to make every guy who booked in here feel good. Because he looked up, gave me a blinding smile—literally, his teeth were whiter than his stark white polo—and eyed me like he appreciated what he saw.

Sorry, Colgate Kid. Not interested.

"Stuart Jenner," I introduced myself. I explained I was

here by myself, and the Colgate Kid gave me what was supposed to be a smouldering look.

I repressed a sigh.

He stood up and walked around the desk to lean against the counter next to me. He was taller than I realised and definitely had a swimmer's physique. Or maybe tennis. Just when I thought he was going to offer something I wasn't interested in, he leaned forward and squinted out the glass wall. "Did you arrive on the White Knight?"

I followed his gaze. "Uh, yeah."

His smile widened. "Is Foster still here?"

I looked at the yacht, then back to the Colgate Kid. "Uh, yeah. Unless he went on foot."

He smiled, and it took me a second to realise I recognised the look on his face. He was hopeful, smitten even.

Jesus. Did Foster have that effect on everyone?

Glad it's not just me then, kid.

I took my room key and found my bungalow. It faced the ocean, separated by a few metres of green grass before meeting white sand and blue water. I set off to explore the grounds and maybe take a stroll before lunch, and I found myself walking up the beach. I really did love it up here. The sand between my toes, the scorching sun, even the humidity. Far North Queensland was like heaven on earth, a million miles away from the dreary stress of my everyday life. I tried not to think about that.

But when I'd walked as far north as the beach would allow, I turned back, and as I neared the resort, I could see the jetty and where the White Knight was still moored. Then I saw Foster walking along the jetty. He wasn't alone. No, not at all. He was walking along with the Colgate Kid, who laughed at something Foster said. They boarded the yacht and disappeared down into the cabin.

My heart squeezed and my stomach dropped when it dawned on me what I was seeing. I knew why Foster was so desperate to be rid of me now.

I felt sick. I felt stupid.

I felt reality drop on me from a great height. Like someone had dumped a bucket of cold water over me, it was shocking, stole my breath, and cleared away any rose-coloured foolish lens I'd been looking through this last week.

CHAPTER FOURTEEN

FOSTER

I DIDN'T WANT Stuart to leave for the day, and I certainly didn't want him to go to the resort and hook up with some other guy.

I did have work things to do that I'd rather him not be on board for, but I didn't want to explain the intricacies of emptying and cleaning out sewer lines. I didn't even like the fact that he washed dishes, though he was adamant to help. But I drew the line at this.

I figured the day apart would do us the world of good, but as I watched him walk off the yacht, I wasn't convinced at all. I'd pretended not to notice that he'd been a little distant as we sailed back to dock. He woke up happy enough, and it was like he shut down as soon as he remembered what he was doing that day.

I could have suggested that if he really didn't want to go to the resort, to just spend the day in Port Douglas. He could spend the day in town, I could do what needed doing, then we could head back out before sunset. I almost suggested it. But Jesus, his trip would be over in another four days, and it wasn't like I'd see him again.

I had to get used to not having him around. I had to get used to that separation, losing that closeness I'd revelled in with him.

I'd really gotten used to having him around.

In just one week.

I'd literally spent the last six years avoiding attachment with anyone. Okay, so maybe not avoiding, but definitely enjoying the fact I spent all my time working at sea and was unable to get attached to anyone.

I didn't want to want anyone.

I didn't want to fall for anyone. I didn't want a relationship. I didn't want to be tied to anyone. I loved being free on the ocean. I'd spent most of my adulthood being tied to a job that almost killed me, wanting nothing except the next contract, the next deadline, the next adrenaline rush.

Now I had simply transferred those reasons—those excuses—into this job. I took one job after the next, sailing all over, never mooring anywhere too long. How did Stuart put it? Did I ever tie my yacht to anyone else's?

No, I did not.

For very good reason. Because the one thing global finance taught me was, the more liabilities you had, the harder the fall.

Investing, trading, selling was for finances. Not for emotions. My heart was not a commodity.

So why did I allow myself to play this game with Stuart?

Because it was just for a short time, a holiday fling of sorts, then he'd be gone, and my life would go back to normal. It was just supposed to be some physical fun. It wasn't supposed to be complicated.

But there was hand holding and soft kisses, gentle touches. I loved the way he smelled, how he tasted, how his body reacted to mine, how he snuggled into me to sleep.

We'd sailed past complicated somewhere around Moore Reef.

So yeah, maybe this day and night apart would do us good.

I stripped beds that smelled of us. I bundled up towels that we'd put on the bed underneath him, that we'd sunbaked on, dried each other with. I bagged up the rubbish that was filled with condom wrappers and sucked-on lemon slices; the empty Corona bottles went to recycling. There were reminders of him everywhere. He'd touched every part of this yacht, and I had to wonder if I'd ever not see the dining table and picture him laughing or if I'd ever use the navigation screens and not smile as I remembered how he tried to use it, or how bare the deck looked without him lazing on it wearing nothing but a smile and those damn white Speedos.

I wondered if I would ever be the same.

———

"FOSTER? YOU IN THERE?" I heard a familiar voice call out.

I stuck my head up the stairs and found Harry standing on the jetty. He was a bright kid who loved anything to do with the water. He was studying marine biology and worked at the resort to pay his way through uni, and he'd often have questions for me whenever I docked here. What kind of fish did I see, what kind of turtles, any whales, any sharks? What were the water temperatures on the reef, did they vary, was anything out of the ordinary?

"Hey, Harry," I said.

His grin widened. "Got any readings for me?"

I chuckled. "Of course. Got a permit for me?"

He produced a folded piece of paper. "Of course."

I grabbed the laundry bag and walked with him back to the resort amenities room. He talked non-stop about his thesis, and the distraction was welcome. After I'd loaded everything into washers, I walked back to the yacht with him, and like always, he came aboard and went through all the data reports he wanted. It was simple really; all my onboard navigation equipment kept records along the plotted course I'd taken. He could simply download what report he wanted and save it to his Google Classroom from his phone.

It took about twenty minutes, and he was back at his desk before his lunch break was over.

I took the permit he'd given me and sailed around to the Port Douglas Marina. I pumped out the head, and tidied up the lines, refuelled, and only had to wait thirty minutes for my grocery delivery to arrive at the marina. I was back at the resort, docked, and had the laundry back on the yacht and the beds remade by the time the sun was getting low.

I'd quite often docked overnight at the resort. I was an LGBT-friendly private charter and this was a gay resort, so it was on the stopover list more often than not. It was how I'd got to know Harry and how I found myself invited to use the restaurant for dinner without being a guest at the resort. It was a nice change to let someone else cook for me, so I took them up on their offer every time.

I waited until the sun was down, showered, then wandered down toward the restaurant. The lights were on at the pool, the bar was busy, music played, and people danced.

I deliberately made myself not think of Stuart or what he was doing or was having done to him right now.

It wasn't my business.

He wasn't my... anything. He was my client.

Actually, while he was off my yacht for these twenty-four hours, he wasn't even that. He wasn't my anything.

Realising that felt like prickles all over my skin. Uncomfortable, almost painful, and really fucking unpleasant. It wasn't supposed to be like this. By the time I sat at a table for one, I'd lost my appetite, and instead of ordering a huge steak, I settled for a seafood grill entree and even had to force that down.

This was such a bad idea.

All of it. Being with him on the yacht like we were lovers was so stupid and unprofessional. But now being here at this club and not being with him felt so much worse. It was pretty obvious though that whatever we had needed to end. When he got back on board tomorrow, if he didn't tell me things were off limits first, then I'd tell him.

I paid for my dinner, and just as I was leaving, a guy approached me. He was a little older than me, and he looked nervous. "You here alone?" he asked.

My heart sank. I didn't want to hurt him when he'd clearly stepped outside of his comfort zone to approach me. "I am," I allowed as we stepped outside, "but I'm not technically staying here for any fun. I'm here on business."

His face fell. "Oh."

"I'm flattered though," I said, giving him what I hoped was a kind smile. I nodded toward the music. "There's a bit of a party happening over at the bar by the sound of it."

"Yeah, not sure that's my scene." He frowned and took a step back. "Thanks anyway."

"Hey, look," I said. "I'll walk over with you, get you to the bar. It's always a little less scary when you don't walk in alone."

He finally smiled. "That's mighty kind of you. I'm David."

"Hi, David," I said as we headed toward the bar. "My name's Foster."

He gave me a brief rundown of his flight from Melbourne, but all I could think while we walked was *please don't let me see Stuart* because I wasn't sure what I'd do if I did. What if he was dancing with another guy? Kissing him? Laughing?

Then I thought, *What if I* don't *see him?*

God, I didn't know which would be worse.

I scanned the crowd at the bar as inconspicuously as I dared and didn't see him anywhere. Yep, it was definitely worse.

I made sure David was at the bar and ordered his first drink, and I even pointed out another guy who was there on his own. When David looked his way, he smiled, so I clapped David on the shoulder and went on my way.

I felt all tight in the chest and my stomach was in knots. This was ridiculous. I'd known him for a fucking week. One fucking week. Now I was cranky for letting myself, Foster Fucking Knight, get attached to something he couldn't have.

I knew better.

As I neared the path to the jetty, I heard familiar laughter coming from the beach. The kind of laugh he let out after a few drinks. I almost stumbled at the sound, tripping over my own feet. But then the laughter ended, followed by, "I don't think so," and "Don't. You can't," and it was Stuart's voice, I had no doubt.

Was he in trouble? He sounded drunk, and before I knew it, I was running through the scrub until I all but fell out onto the beach. "Hey!"

There were three figures about twenty metres up the

beach. I picked Stuart out easily, his stance, his swagger. There was enough moonlight for me to see his face, and his smile died when he saw it was me.

He wasn't in trouble at all. One of the guys he was with had something in his hand and Stuart and the third guy were looking at it.

"Everything okay here?" I asked, realising I was interrupting something that was none of my business. Stuart didn't need my help. He didn't need me at all.

Stuart threw his arm out. "What the fuck is it to you?"

Yep, he was definitely drunk.

"Do you know this guy?" one of the guys asked.

"Yep. Sure do," he replied.

I put my hand up with my heart in my throat. "Sorry. I thought there might have been some trouble."

The taller of the other guys put his arm around the other guy in a protective way, and I wondered if they were a couple who'd maybe asked Stuart to join them. He'd obviously said yes.

I stepped back, making my retreat, but apparently Stuart wasn't done. "Why would you care?" he yelled across the beach. "I saw you. Don't pretend to fucking care when you don't."

I stopped. *Saw me?* "What? I said I thought you might have been in trouble."

Stuart waved his hand back at the couple who were now watching us, and he staggered a bit, obviously very drunk. "Found a seashell. Told him he couldn't take it. Wouldn't call it trouble, though the fun police has arrived," he said, making a siren sound. One of the guys chuckled.

I took another step back. "Sorry. Enjoy your night."

I turned to leave but Stuart's yelling stopped me. "I saw

you, arsehole. Don't pretend to be all high and mighty with me now."

Saw me do what? I took a step toward him and yelled back, "Saw me do what? I don't know what you're talking about!"

Stuart scoffed and waved me off. Then he spun back to me and pointed at his own chest as he yelled again. "You think I don't care? Well, guess what? I don't. I don't give a shit about who you fuck."

The other two guys must have realised this was personal because they backed off and left me and Stuart on the beach alone. "Who I fuck?" I repeated, walking toward him. "What the hell are you talking about?"

"I saw you! You couldn't wait to kick me off your boat so you could what? Fuck the Colgate Kid? On my bed? Or yours?"

"The Colgate Kid?" I shook my head. "What the fuck are you talking about?"

"The pretty blond receptionist," he spat at me. "I saw you with him. I watched you make him laugh, then take him on board."

What? "Harry?"

"Oh, is that his name? Was he good? He was waiting for you when I booked in." Then he jabbed his finger at my chest. "You told me you were single. You told me you had no one. That there was no one."

"There isn't!"

"I saw you take him on board!" He staggered back a little. "And he didn't leave for half an hour. What were you doing? It doesn't take a rocket scientist to figure that out."

"You're drunk."

His eyes gleamed. "You're a fucking liar."

Now I was angry. "I did not lie to you. I never lied. I

didn't do anything with Harry. Jesus, Stuart. He's a fucking kid. He's studying marine biology. He takes recordings from my navigation system on water temps up and down the reef. Printouts, Stuart. And he lets me use the laundry room here."

He narrowed his eyes at me. "You didn't..."

"No! He's a kid, Stuart. Jesus."

He looked defeated, then sparked up again. "Then why did you want me off the boat so bad today?"

"Because I had to empty the sewer tank and clean the lines."

"Oh." Then he made a face. "Ew. That's gross."

I laughed at that, the fight between us over.

"You could have just told me that," he said, pouting. "Saved me drinking all that tequila to teach you a lesson."

I snorted. "And how's that working out for you?"

"Okay right now, but tomorrow's gonna suck."

"Probably."

"Greasy breakfast and a swim in salt water will fix me right up." He leaned and took a step to correct himself. "Know of any private yachts I could charter?"

I barked out a laugh. "Maybe. Do you... do you want me to help you back to your room?"

He turned around, looking around the beach like he had no memory of getting there, then pointed to some cabins facing the ocean. "Number ten."

I put my arm around him and tried to help him up onto the grassy ledge off the beach. "Just how much tequila did you drink?"

"Enough to teach you a lesson."

I laughed again and took his hand. It was easier to pull him along than herd him. We got to the door and Stuart came to a stop behind me, goofy expression on his face, swaying on his feet. "Give me the key, Mr Alquimia."

He cocked his head, dopey smile still in place. "Mr what?"

"Mr Tequila."

"Oh." Then he laughed. "You're funny."

"Key?"

"'S in my pocket." He made no attempt to get it out, so I patted him down, finding the key in his back pocket. "You like my arse," he slurred.

"Yes, I do." I swiped the key card and opened the door, pulling him inside. I hit the light switch and turned just in time to catch Stuart before he swayed too far left. "Whoa there, tequila man."

He fell against me. His eyes were swimming, unfocused, his breath sweet. "'M sorry 'bout before."

"About what?"

"Thinking you and the Colgate Kid..."

I snorted. "The Colgate Kid? Really?"

Stuart gave me a grin that became a grimace that showed all his teeth. Then he waved a hand at his face and squinted. "Teeth blinded me."

"He's a nice kid. But he *is* a kid. And, just so you know, I will accept your apology, after we've discussed this more tomorrow." I led him to the huge bed and pushed him onto it. He sprawled out, face down, with a laugh.

"Like it when you play rough."

I pulled his shoes off and dropped them to the floor. "You need sleep."

He rolled onto his side, then onto his back with what appeared to be great effort. "I didn't do nothing with those guys. You need to know that."

I nodded. "Okay."

"Foster," he slurred, raising one hand. "You need to know I didn't."

"I know."

"Do you? Really know, Foster? Cause I don't want nobody but you."

"Is that so?" I asked. He was drunk, so I didn't want to take anything he said too seriously. Or did he need the alcohol to inhibit his filter? Maybe he was the type who spoke his mind when he was drunk.

"Mmhmm," he assented. "Stay with me tonight."

"I can't."

He frowned and closed his eyes. "I didn't do nothin' with those guys."

I put my hand on his leg and pulled the sheet over him. "I know. I can't stay because of the resort's company policy."

He mumbled something that sounded like *stupid*. Then he rolled onto his side, his eyes still closed. "Can I tell you something?" he whispered.

I wasn't sure if I really wanted to hear this or really didn't. "Sure."

I waited, and I waited a little longer. Then he began to snore. I scrubbed my hand over my face, looked at him sound asleep and snoring, and laughed. I put a glass of water beside his bed, turned the lights off, walked out, and locked the door behind me.

EIGHT O'CLOCK THE NEXT MORNING, I knocked a little louder than was probably necessary, and I heard a grunted response. The door opened and Stuart stood there, looking a little worse for wear, but at least he was awake.

Showered and dressed too. He looked at my face, then at the two coffees I was holding. "Oh, thank God. Please tell me one of those is mine."

I handed him one. "I wasn't expecting you to be up."

"The bed kept rocking. I feel like I'm on the boat."

I snorted. "Pretty sure tequila will do that."

He groaned, then sipped his coffee, making a face. "Christ. Did Satan make this?"

"Yep. Ground from the beans of where hopes and dreams go to die."

He smiled as he tried another sip. "Sounds about right. It's bitter as fuck."

I fought a smile. Stuart obviously didn't do hangovers very well. "I asked for extra strong. Figured you'd need it."

"I need food."

"Come on then, let's get you fed."

We walked to the restaurant, which now had a buffet breakfast spread out. There were a few people out and about, but Stuart chose a table by the window away from everyone, though as soon as he sat down, he put his sunnies on. He shrugged at me. "I want the sun, not the glare. It's burning my brain."

I chuckled at him. "You're pitiful. Get something to eat, for God's sake."

I opted for bacon and fruit, and he loaded his plate full of everything on offer. "This will either fix me or put me back in bed," he mumbled. We were quiet while he shovelled in the first few mouthfuls, then once he slowed down, he sat back and sighed. "Sorry about last night."

I sipped my coffee and waited a moment, holding his gaze. "You apologised last night."

He pushed his sunnies to the top of his head and stared right back at me. "And you said we'd talk about it today."

"You remember?"

He nodded. "Yeah. I am sorry. I assumed something about you that was out of line."

"Yes, you did."

"I just saw you take that kid on board your boat and figured... I mean, he's a good-looking kid."

"Despite the blinding smile?"

Stuart snorted and ate some more, and a line appeared between his eyebrows like he was thinking of something. "You found me on the beach with those guys. I met them at the bar, but I didn't..." He shook his head.

"You told me you didn't. I believe you." I let out a deep breath. "Not that I have any kind of claim on you, so you could have if you wanted to."

"I didn't want to," he said quickly. "I mean, I was pissed and hurt because I thought you had that kid on your boat, and..."

"And?"

"And it should have been me." A sweet pink stained his cheeks. "I thought you'd booted me off so you could have him."

I liked his honesty. I liked that he could say what he meant, even if it wasn't easy. I folded my linen serviette, put it on the table, and decided to give him my truth in return. "Stuart, here's the thing. In the six years I've been doing this private charter thing, I could count on one hand the number of guys I've been with. What we've been doing... well, I've never done anything like it before. But this last week has been—" I paused to search for the right word.

"Incredible?" he offered.

I nodded. "Incredible."

He licked his bottom lip. "What does it mean? For us, I

mean. I have three days left, and I'd really like for things to go back to how they were before I..."

"Tried to drown yourself in tequila?"

He snorted and his lips made a thin, watery line. "God, don't remind me."

I sighed loudly, not even trying to hide the disappointment in my voice. "Three days, huh?"

Stuart's gaze locked with mine and he nodded, but before either of us could speak, Harry appeared from nowhere, dragged a seat over from a nearby table, and sat down. "Foster, I'm so glad you're still here," he said, holding some papers. Then he straightened and looked at each of us in turn. "Hope I'm not interrupting."

I smiled at this kid's enthusiasm. "Harry, I'd like you to meet Stuart. Stuart, Harry."

"Oh, hi." Harry gave Stuart one of his killer-watt grins and Stuart sat back and pulled his sunglasses back down.

"Hey."

I sipped my coffee to hide my smile, and Harry held out the papers for me to look at. "With the data I've collected from you, I've found an average of a zero point three degree increase in sea temperatures over the last two years..."

He spoke non-stop for five minutes straight about how he'd already been in touch with some government office this morning with his findings, and the turtle conservation organisation was taking his information real serious, and how, with thanks to me, his thesis was gonna be lit.

I just assumed *lit* was a good thing but didn't interrupt.

Stuart was still wearing his sunglasses, though his mouth opened and closed a few times as though he had serious concerns for Harry's ability to talk and breathe at the same time. Then Harry told us how excited he was that his university's aquamarine department was about to release some baby turtles and we should totally go and watch. And then, another staff member caught his attention. "Hey, Judy!" he said, and with as much enthusiasm, and all in the one breath, he said goodbye to us and was telling Judy all about his findings as they walked out of the restaurant, his papers in his hand.

I watched him leave, and when I turned back to Stuart, he was pushing his sunnies back up. A stunned look on his face. "Wow."

I laughed. "Told ya. He's a good kid. He'll spend his life saving the world."

Stuart finished his coffee. "I can see now, he's really not your type."

I smiled at him. "Yeah, I prefer the tall, dark, and brooding type." Then I leaned across the table. "Guys who get all bent out of shape over nothing, drink far too much tequila, and like to be fucked into the mattress."

Stuart's nostrils flared. "Which you didn't do last night, I might add. I seem to recall being face down on the bed and you walking out."

"Because you were drunk."

He inhaled deeply. "Just as well my type is the sailing type with morals then, isn't it?"

I fought a smile. "Yes, just as well." Then I remembered something. "About last night, you said 'Hey, can I tell you something?' but passed out before you did. What did you want to tell me?"

He stared me right in the eyes and chewed on the inside of his lip. "I don't remember."

It made me laugh. "Liar."

He chuckled and dropped his serviette over his plate. "I'm ready to go. You ready to go?"

"Yep. So, did the breakfast fix you? Or will you be spending the day in bed?"

He smirked. "Yes, and yes. You can sail us to somewhere remote where there's not another soul in sight, then do to me all day long what you didn't do last night."

Warmth pooled low in my belly. "You check out of your room. I'll meet you on the yacht."

CHAPTER FIFTEEN

STUART

I BOARDED the yacht and went straight down to my cabin, noted the freshly made bed, the subtle smell of lemon disinfectant, and smiled. I was comfortable here; the confined space felt like a cocoon. A really well-designed, expensive cocoon.

I unpacked my bag, happy to not be leaving. For three days, anyway.

I didn't want to think about leaving. I didn't want to go back to my old life, my old job. The thought of wearing a suit and even socks and shoes and, God forbid, a damn necktie, made me feel claustrophobic. I considered taking my phone out while we had good reception but decided not to.

I had three days left. I was damn well going to enjoy them.

I found Foster at the stern, doing some fancy thing with the rope. Sorry, tying off the dock line. I doubted I'd ever get used to nautical terminology. I had no need to, I guess.

"You ready to go?" he asked, his grin wide.

"Hell yes. I want to see nothing but sunshine and blue

water for the next three days. No other people, if we can manage it."

Foster laughed. "Well, we're heading to the Low Isles. There will be people. I can't avoid that, but we can anchor off the east side where not many people go."

"Excellent. Can we swim and snorkel there?"

"Yep." He got in behind the wheel. "Okay, now come stand here with me," he said. "We have to use engine power, obviously, and you're going to do it."

"Me?"

"Yep."

"But... there are boats." I gestured broadly to the ocean.

He grinned. "It's not that busy. You'll be fine."

"But—"

"Don't argue with the captain. A cabin boy must do what he's told."

I rolled my eyes and walked over to him. He positioned me at the wheel, his arms around my shoulders so we could both steer. I could feel his entire body at my back. "This isn't so bad," I allowed. "Do good cabin boys get rewards?"

He chuckled and nudged the back of my head with his nose. But then he was all business about sailing and teaching me, guiding me how to do it. As soon as we were out in open water, he cut the engine. "Now, go read the chart-plotter and tell me what to do," he ordered.

Ugh. This again.

I marked in our destination, the Low Isles, as he'd said, and relayed the following information. "Wind direction is nor'easter, at ten knots. Point of sail is... close hauled, I think."

Foster grinned. "And the VMG?"

"Seven point eight."

He lifted his face to the wind, his smile serene. "So, mainsail or jib?"

"Um..." I looked up at the mast like it could somehow give me the answer. "Both?"

"You totally guessed that."

"One hundred per cent."

He laughed. "Go take the sail cover off like I showed you."

"Yes, captain." I stepped along the deck to the sail and did everything he'd shown me. I made my way back to the cockpit and did the line winch like he'd done a dozen times. He made it all look so damn easy.

I couldn't remember the exact terminology for everything, but I knew what to do. Well, I think I did. I noticed Foster standing idle, smiling at me. "How'd I do?"

He grinned and gave me a thumbs up. "Perfect. Now do the jib."

He watched as I did what I remembered, wrapping the line around the winch and unfurling the sail. But, with all the patience under the sun, he explained that must always run on top of the spinnaker pole and in front of the topping lift. And I nodded like I was supposed to understand.

He laughed in the sunlight and gave my hand a squeeze. "Get back behind the wheel."

"Will you stand behind me like you did before?" I asked seriously.

He just laughed, and when I was back behind the wheel, he sat right beside me, his hand touching the inside of my knee. He was the picture of relaxed, feet extended, legs crossed at the ankle, a peaceful smile on his face, the wind in his hair. "I could get used to this," he said. "Being chauffeured around the Whitsundays every day."

"Well, don't get too used to it," I said. "There's a boat off the right—"

"Starboard," he corrected, but he peered around me, his hand now on my waist. "They're two miles away, Stuart."

"Yeah, well, don't expect me to know what the hell I'm doing if they get too close. Can I just yell at them to move?"

He snorted. "Doesn't exactly work that way."

"Well, it should. Do you want to drive now?"

"Nope." He leaned back and slid his hand around my leg again and closed his eyes. "You got this all under control."

And so we stayed like that for quite a while: him pretending to rest, looking up every so often, and me pretending to know how to sail. But soon enough, a shimmer on the horizon solidified into land. "Ah, Captain?"

"Hmm?"

"Land ahoy."

Foster shot to his feet and squeezed in behind me again, and he navigated us around the southern point of the island. It was a few islands, actually, but the biggest, Low Island, was about two hectares in size, or so Foster said. There was an inlet on the northern side, a small harbour that was popular and busy during the day where we could drop anchor if the wind picked up. But for the whole day, we'd sit east of the island where others tended not to go. There were reefs to snorkel, but it wasn't perfect, he'd said.

But the fact there was no one else there meant it was perfect for us.

We anchored, swam and snorkelled, sunbaked, and made out, kissing on the deck like teenagers. I was on my back, and he was on his front, our lips locked in lazy, tender kisses. When Foster palmed my erection, he smiled against my mouth. "You're obviously feeling a lot better."

"Much."

He bit his lip. "How much better?"

I caught his intention. That heated look in his eyes was a dead giveaway. "Well, I could feel a whole lot better," I said with a smirk.

"Yeah, how so?"

"Pretty sure a thorough fucking would fix me, good and proper."

He laughed and pushed up onto his feet, but my eyes went to his dick as he gave himself a squeeze. He held out his hand. "Then let's not keep you waiting."

He led me down into his room this time, and something was different. He was different. It wasn't fraught grabbing, desperate pushing and pulling. It was slow and measured, his touch soft and tender. He laid me on his bed, stretching me with gentle fingers, kissing me, languid and lovely, until I was putty in his hands.

He moulded me, pliable and wanting, and when he was finally inside me, there was no fucking me into the mattress. I was on my back, my knees pressed up near my chest, and he was so far inside me, holding my face, kissing me so deeply, devouring me, while he filled me so completely.

This was slow and deep, reaching places inside me no one had ever dared.

He was making love to me.

Every thrust was for my pleasure. Every caress was to make me feel good, every kiss to show me how much he wanted me.

He wrung my orgasm out of me, like a tortured bliss bomb, then he held me while I unravelled underneath him. And he thrust in so, so deep one last time, flexing every muscle as he came, his face contorted in the most beautiful way.

He collapsed on me, and we lay there for the longest time. Neither one of us wanted to move. I traced circles on his back, and he sighed before pulling back so he could kiss me.

Oh, yeah. This was definitely different.

Something had changed between us. Kind of scary and amazing. Something I couldn't name; something I didn't want to examine too closely. I just wanted to hold him and have him hold me and kiss me like he was right now.

I thought he might get up and go check upstairs that everything was as it should be. But he didn't. Not right then, anyway. We stayed in bed. We ate lunch in bed. We kissed and laughed and made love again.

By the time it was late afternoon, we swam again. Then we sat on the bench seat in the cockpit, me between his legs, my back to his chest. Instead of sailing into the inlet, we stayed right where we were, and with his arms strong around me, we watched the sunset.

When the last of the light turned the orange sky to purple, he kissed the side of my head. "Today has been perfect."

I turned in his arms. "Yes, it has. I don't want it to end." I probably didn't mean to admit so much, but he'd unlocked something in me.

"Then let me take you back to bed," he replied, kissing me with a passion, a tenderness that surprised me. "And we'll make it last all night."

THE NEXT DAY we woke up early with plans to sail around to the inlet and walk the beach while no one else was around. But we sat in the cockpit and ate our breakfast, and we saw dolphins in the distance, stingrays and turtles off the reef. It was so beautiful, so secluded—there were no other boats around this side of the island. There was no beach, as such, just rocky outcrops, so tourists generally had no reason to stop here. We ended up swimming off the back of the yacht, snorkelling with tropical fish and it was so beautiful, we decided to stay put. The fact that no one else was around made it perfect. There was no one to burst our private bubble. The sun was belting us though, and the humidity thick, so we spent the morning alternating between swimming and drying off in the cockpit.

"Shit, it's hot," I complained, sweating in the shade of the cockpit. We'd been diving in the water just to cool off and were almost sweating again before we could reach for a towel when we got out.

Foster looked up, then toward the north. "Might rain later. The humidity has to be in the nineties."

I wiped my brow and grabbed us a bottle of water each. "Here, keep your fluids up."

He gulped half it down, and even he looked a little frazzled. "You know, we could spend the day in the cabin, shut the door and turn the air conditioning on."

I stared at him. "You have air conditioning?"

He chuckled. "Of course I do."

"Then what the hell are we doing sweating our arses off up here?"

"When I could be making you sweat below deck."

I grinned. "Exactly. Sweating in the air-conditioned below deck is way more my cup of tea."

Foster shut everything down, made sure everything was good, followed me below deck, and closed the door behind us. "I should just check the weather," he said, pulling up some screen. It was a radar map and there was a band of green moving down the coast of Queensland. "Yeah, between ten and fifteen millimetres expected this afternoon. That explains the humidity. It's at eighty-nine."

"What does that mean for us?" I asked. "We've had nothing but sunshine and gentle breezes. What does rain mean out here?"

"That if you stand in it, you get wet." He smirked. "No, nothing. Fifteen mil is nothing. As long as the wind doesn't pick up, we're good. If it does, we'll just sail around to the inlet. It's nothing to worry about. And anyway, if it does rain, it just means we'll have to find something to do for a few hours down here."

"Hmm," I hummed, smiling at him. "Any suggestions? Cards, crosswords, sudoku perhaps?"

He strode over to me and pushed me against the galley cabinet, pinning me with his hips. His smile was devilish. "Oh, I have much better plans for you."

His words, his tone, the lust in his eyes, set my blood on fire. How was it possible that I wanted more? We'd had so much sex, we should be chaffed and aching. My arse should be sore, but it wasn't. I wanted more. Everything he could give me, I'd take. Willingly. Hell, I'd even beg for it. My balls drew up at the thought of him taking me again, sliding inside me, trying to become one with me.

My body wanted him like he was oxygen.

This time, he had me on the table. I was on my back, my arse at his hips, his cock buried inside me. He kissed me, stroked me, held me, making me see fireworks behind my eyelids as my orgasm ripped through me. He gripped my hips hard when he came, and I could feel him swell and pulse deep, so deep as he filled the condom.

When we could both move and our senses had returned, we were both exhausted and he dragged me into his bed for a nap. "I thought yesterday was perfect," I said as he wrapped me up in his arms. "But today might win."

He nuzzled into me, giving the back of my head sleepy kisses. "It's a tie," he mumbled. "But today is far from over. The best might be yet to come."

I WOKE BEFORE FOSTER, so I decided to surprise him with a late lunch. I made a quick chicken salad, tore up some bread, and added a small bowl of olive oil and balsamic, and added some fruit on the side. I poured us some juice and noticed he'd bought some oysters. I wasn't a fan, but he wanted them last time we went grocery shopping but decided against them. He clearly decided in their favour this time because there was a dozen, already shucked. So, I added them to the tray.

I slid the tray on the bed, rousing him from sleep. And we sat there in the cool air conditioning feeding each other forkfuls of salad and dunking bread in oil and vinegar. "I didn't know what to do with the oysters," I said. "So I just left them plain."

"Perfect. That's how I love them." He took one, tipped the shell, and let the oyster slide down his throat.

I shook my head. "You can keep them. Not that you need them," I laughed. "Well, not the aphrodisiac aspect. You don't need any help in that department."

He laughed and downed one more. "Have you ever had them before?"

"Only with vodka and chilli."

"Ah, that's where you went wrong."

"They weren't that bad," I admitted. "Just not my

favourite. I'll stick to carbs and fats." I dunked another chunk of bread and ate it, licking the oil off my finger.

"I know the view outside is absolutely priceless, but the air conditioning in here was a much better idea," I said. We stayed like that, leaning against the headboard, half sitting up, half lying down, the blankets pulled to our waists. It was so much more comfortable than the stifling humidity outside. "I could get used to this."

A few minutes of what I thought was an easy silence, Foster looked a little uncomfortable. Like he was trying to figure out how to ask me something. "You can just say it, you know."

He frowned. "Say what?"

"Whatever it is you want to ask me or tell me."

He swallowed hard. "No, I just..."

"Wanted to ask me if I was really going to go back to my old life?"

He shot me a look.

"I have to," I answered without him saying anything. "I have responsibilities. I can't just walk away, as much as I might want to."

He didn't say anything, so I distracted myself by eating a few grapes. "I mean, this break has been the best thing that I can remember, if I'm being honest. And I'm sure I'll go back to Brisbane in a better frame of mind than when I got here. I don't really want to go back; I'd love to stay right here forever. But I have to. Actually, when I get back, I'm heading straight to Sydney. If my associates haven't fucked up the final paperwork of the biggest contract I ever worked on."

Foster hadn't said a word, and when I looked at him, I expected to see sadness or even anger, but his face was twisted in something else. "Fine," I joked. "I'll try an oyster. It's for your benefit if either of us needs an aphrodisiac."

I picked up an oyster, readying myself, but he reached out, and with a hand on my arm, he stopped me. "Don't eat it."

I looked at his face and realised it was discomfort.

He wasn't just pale. He was green.

Oh no.

He bolted off the bed and ran for the bathroom. I heard him vomit into the toilet, and I knew, it was common knowledge, that food poisoning from oysters wasn't good. I followed him in. "Holy shit. Are you okay?"

He was bent over the bowl, still naked, heaving into the toilet. He put his hand up like he was telling me to leave him be. I grabbed a hand towel and ran it under cold water, and when he stopped being sick and leaned back, I handed him the towel and he wiped his face. He looked god-awful. "Hop back into bed," I suggested.

I helped him to his feet. He was shaky, clammy, but I held his elbow, and when we got back into his room, I sat him down, then cleared the bed of the food I'd brought in.

By the time I'd put the tray on the galley counter, he was back in the bathroom being sick in the toilet again.

I gave him a minute, then followed him in. "Hey."

He was now sitting on the floor, his back against the wall. He was kind of slumped, still naked, and still a shade of green I'd never seen on a human before. He raised his hand again, then let it fall to his lap. "Ugh," he groaned. "Not good." He groaned again, then launched up to vomit again.

He wasn't leaving the bathroom any time soon. He was ill and I needed to look after him, take charge. I rinsed out the towel again, wringing it, and gave it back to him when he sat back.

He *really* wasn't leaving the bathroom any time soon. I went back to his room, grabbed a pillow and pulled a sheet off the bed, and took them back to him. He was more slumped than before. "Here," I said gently. "Lie down. I'll be back." I put the sheet over him, not that he probably cared at that point, but my concern was for him, not to ogle him while he was sick.

I threw all the food on the tray into the bin and cleaned everything I could. I heard Foster be sick a few more times, and I had no clue what else to do. I didn't know what to expect, what to give him, or just how bad it could get. I took Foster's tablet, which I'd seen him use before to look up weather reports, so I knew it had an internet connection. I found the Google icon and quickly searched food poisoning and oysters, looking for ailments and whatever I could do to help him and what to expect. Just how sick was he going to get, and how long would it last?

Four Google searches later, and according to Dr Google, he'd either be fine in a few hours or die a painful death. Fuck. I should know better than to Google anything medical, but at least I knew what to do. Fluids, check temperature, and call for medical help if things got worse; common sense, really. Given the fact he'd vomited so quickly, and so thoroughly, after eating them was a blessing.

The yacht was moving a lot more than I was used to. Maybe him being sick was making things seem worse than they were. Maybe my equilibrium was off because I was worried. The machines near the radio were beeping more than usual. Or did they always beep like that and I didn't notice? I'd never paid attention to them before because I'd never had to.

Goddammit. *Stop panicking, Stuart.*

I found some Lucozade in the fridge and took it into the bathroom. He was curled up on the floor, his eyes closed, his head on the pillow, the sheet half pulled over him. He would have looked kind of peaceful if he wasn't green.

"Foster?" I spoke quietly.

He groaned.

I took a step in and held up the plastic tumbler. "I need you to drink this."

He groaned his dissent.

"It will help."

He opened his eyes, so I knelt beside him and held the cup to his lips. He sipped a little and made a face, and after a long, undecided moment, he sat up so he could vomit again into the toilet.

Then a crack of thunder boomed overhead like it had reached out and shook the mast. "Fuck!" I cried, running through the cabin. I pushed on the door and burst outside to a dark and stormy sky, low rumbling clouds, and the rear flag was flapping in the wind.

Fuck!

I went up into the cockpit, noticing the movement of the yacht so much more up there. I had to hold on as we bobbed in the water. I looked out across the water. There were no other boats in sight, the trees on the island swayed heavily, and because things weren't bad enough right now, the clouds opened and dumped a deluge of rain.

I grabbed what I could and threw the stuff into the under-seat storage. Anything that was movable or not bolted down went in there, and by the time I went back downstairs, I was drenched right through and the swell was worse. The yacht now rocked like a cork in the ocean.

And it dawned on me, like the clouds a minute ago, like

a fucking torrential downpour: I was on a yacht in the middle of the fucking ocean with an incapacitated skipper, and I had no clue, absolutely none, of what to do.

I raced to the bathroom to ask Foster, but he was leaning over the toilet, dry retching into the bowl. His whole body heaved, the muscles in his back stretched and slid under his skin. I hated noticing this about him in a time like this. "Uh, Foster?"

He slid back to the floor and groaned.

"There's a storm," I added.

His eyes closed and he moaned. The green-grey pallor of his skin wasn't a good sign. I took the face washer, rinsed it again and wiped his forehead, the rest of his face, just as more thunder boomed and lightning split the sky outside. We were rocking solidly now, a sensation I doubted Foster could even feel. But there was no rhythm to it; it was jagged and jostling.

Fuck, fuck, fuck.

Okay, so I was doing this by myself.

I realised then that Foster's machines were beeping and flashing, but I had no clue what to make of it. He'd tried to explain it to me briefly, and I remembered him talking about communications and weather updates, but I hadn't paid enough attention. I wasn't expecting to have to know this...

I grabbed the navigation screen and searched the weather radar. And holy shit. There was a huge band of red, yellow, and white coming in from the east. And we were sitting on the east side of the island, on the east side of the reef.

I didn't know much about sailing, but I knew that wasn't good.

We were right in its path.

What could I do? Just sit here, helpless, bobbing around

like a toy boat in a turbulent bathtub? What if the seas got so rough we capsized? Was that even possible on a reef? I recalled Foster saying the water was deeper on this side of the island, but we'd stayed here because I'd wanted to avoid human interaction. Jesus. We were around here, on the wrong side of the island, because of me. And Foster was deathly ill.

It wasn't like I could do anything. Could I?

The yacht was now swaying. Things in cupboards were starting to move, slide. I braced myself behind the table so I wouldn't fall over, or be injured should something fall on me.

I clicked on Google, not knowing what the hell to even search, and started with the basics. It would have been almost laughable if I wasn't so damn scared.

Sailing in a storm.

Did I pull up anchor? Did I set the sails and hope to blow out of the path of it? Did I sit tight and leave it in the hands of the gods?

I read the first few posts, and surprisingly enough, found a few actual 'what to do' sites and what they said kind of made sense...

I checked the weather map again. The worst of the storm wasn't even close, and from what I could tell, we were in the worst possible spot for impact.

I had to do something.

Then a crackling noise scared the crap out of me. "This is QF10 Coast Guard, Port Douglas. White Knight, please respond. White Knight, White Knight, please respond."

White Knight. That's us! The two-way radio thing! There was someone speaking to us! I managed to get to the radio despite the movement of the boat, grabbed the mouthpiece, and pressed the button. I had no clue about nautical or naval radio protocol. "Hello?"

"White Knight, please respond. Over."

"This is White Knight."

Silence.

Oh. "Over," I added.

"Foster Knight? Confirm. Over."

"No. My name is Stuart Jenner. I'm a passenger on board the White Knight. Foster is sick. He has food poisoning." Then silence. Shit. "Over."

"Is it life threatening? Do you require a rescue helicopter? Over."

"No, I don't think so..." He ate some bad oysters but a rescue helicopter like in the movies was a little drastic, wasn't it?

"Do you know your location. Over."

He probably wanted GPS coordinates, but that was information I couldn't give him. "We were on the east coast of some island. Um, the Low Islands or something, I can't remember. Over."

"Is your vessel secure? Over."

"I don't know what you mean by secure. I've put everything on the deck into storage, but it's getting kinda rough. We're moving around a lot. I was just wondering if I should haul the anchor in? Or try to sail around to the inlet Foster mentioned." Silence. "Oh, over."

"Are you capable of sailing the vessel? Is there probable risk to life? Over."

Fuck. "I don't know..." I scrubbed my hand over my face as real fear began to claw at my insides. I could hear Foster trying to be sick again, but his stomach was well past empty.

"White Knight, please respond."

"Oh. Shit. Sorry. Over. I don't know how this is supposed to work."

"We can have a Coast Guard boat to you in seventy-five minutes. Please confirm. Over."

And it struck me—be it stupidity and a flawed bravado or belief in myself—but in seventy-five minutes, it could all be over. I couldn't just sit on my hands and wait for a wave to drive us to smithereens. I had to do something. "No. I'll sail us into the inlet. Over."

"Please repeat. Over."

"I'll sail us into the inlet. We'll be safer there. Over." And this time when I said it, it came out with more conviction. I hung up the receiver and remembered Foster harping on about safety protocol and where the floatation device belts were. I pulled up the seating cushion and, still swaying with the rough seas, pulled out two of those stupid waist belt floatation things. I clipped mine on easy, but I knew Foster's would be a different story. I made my way into the bathroom, bracing myself against the doorway. Foster was curled into a ball on the floor, almost curling around the toilet. Jesus. He was also more grey than green now and I didn't know if that was a good or bad thing, and he was also naked but the sheet was tangled around him.

"Okay, I need you to put this on," I said, stepping into the room, holding the shower wall and basin for support from the rocking of the yacht. I bent over him, trying to brace myself between the walls with my feet, and tried sliding one end underneath him, but I couldn't get it. "Foster, baby, I need you to try and sit up."

He opened his eyes and groaned.

"Can you sit up a bit?"

He tried to move, so I helped by heaving him up by the shoulder. He was dead weight and moaning like the movement made him sick. I pulled on his arm, probably rougher than I should have, and quickly clipped the belt on around his waist but at least he now had it on. Foster went back to the floor and I lifted his head, more gently than I'd afforded his arm, and shoved the pillow under him, and he fought to curl up again. I finally got him settled before he rolled back up onto his knees and was sick in the toilet. He was now down to green bile, and I knew from far too much cheap wine in my uni days how horrible that was.

When he was done and curled back up on the floor, I took the washer and wiped his face. "Thank you," he mumbled.

I pounced on his moment of clarity. "Foster, I'm going to try and sail us around through the inlet." Thunder cracked overhead. "The storm'll hit us too hard here."

He looked at me with bleary eyes and sank back to the floor. I covered him again with the sheet and looked around. He was actually quite well insulated in the bathroom. He couldn't really hurt himself too much from the floor, but I went back out and grabbed the seat cushions and wedged them around him for good measure.

The boat was rocking steadily now and we seemed to be rocking side to side, not bow to stern, which told me the boat was kinda facing the wrong way. I pushed the door to the cockpit open, though it tried to hold in the wind. I shoved it hard and made my way up, only to kind of wish I hadn't.

The sky was darker than I remembered. The wind was stronger, the waves were bigger, rain hammered in on a slant. I couldn't see past the edge of the yacht.

Fuck.

I looked over the coach housing toward the bow. The sails were down, thankfully. I'd hate to imagine where we'd be if they were still up. But Foster had dropped anchor when we got here, and I knew I should pull it in so I hit the button to pull the anchor up, but the whir of the line hauling in sounded wrong, strung and fraught.

Fuck!

From the way the water was pushing against us, the anchor line must be stuck, holding us so we were going against the waves.

Hammered by rain, and holding on to the railing line as tight as I could, I made it to the anchor. I tried looking over the side of the yacht to see if I could see anything obvious, and yeah, it was pulled tight against the boat.

Fuck.

The last thing I needed to happen was to snap it or for it to snag and pull the side of the yacht down. I went to the wheel and turned us into the anchor line, trying to give it more room. The wind pushed, the waves pulled, the rain bucketed down, but shifting our angle had swung us back a little. Just enough. The line yanked and began to retract, free from whatever had held it.

Then I remembered Foster telling me he'd once hit a Category 2 storm. Was that what this was? A Category 2?

I tried not to think of that.

But he hadn't gone into specifics, and I didn't think to ask. It was information I shouldn't need to have known!

Okay, take a breath, Stuart.

I needed to keep my head on. And I needed to get my bearings.

Every time lightning lit the sky, I could see the island to my left, but it was more at seven o'clock and I needed it at nine. North was twelve o'clock and I needed to go north to the top of the island. I swung the wheel, trying to bring us around, but it was against the waves. We were hitting the swells side-on, but if I turned the bow into the storm, we'd go nowhere. If I turned the bow away from the storm, we'd run aground into the island. I needed to keep the wind on my starboard side, as wrong as it felt.

I had no clue what I was doing.

The wind drove rain into my face, and I was soaked through to the bone. My hands shook. My whole body shook. It wasn't cold, I was scared out of my mind. But I turned the key, and as water, rain, and waves pelted the dashboard, I saw the gauges crank to life.

I didn't realise I'd half expected the engine not to work. I couldn't hear the quiet hum of the engine over the storm, but the gauges told me it was running. Shit! Wasn't I supposed to pull the anchor in after I turned the engine over? *Too late now!* Thunder boomed, sheets of lightning lit up the darkening sky, scaring the shit out of me. But it somehow made me focus, and I pretended, like I'd always pretended, that I knew how to sail.

The truth was, I had no clue how to sail.

I'd held onto the wheel when Foster was in charge, like how a kid might hold the steering wheel of a car, perched up on their dad's lap.

I had no clue how fast I was going, no clue how fast I was supposed to go. I pushed on the throttle, not all the way. As much as I wanted to floor it and speed to escape this nightmare, I knew safe and steady was best.

We lurched up on a wave, and I thought the other side was gone. We seemed to fall forever, but we landed with a thud, carving into rough water at the wrong angle.

Jesus. Was I going to get us smashed to pieces?

Then we lurched forward, and all I could do was keep the darkness of the island on my left. Not too close, not too far. I didn't know how far away the reef was to my right. I didn't know how far north I had to go. All I could do was stumble forward and try to hold the yacht steady. The wind and the water were pushing, shoving, screaming us into the island, but it was rocky outcrops, it was reefs and coral, shallows, and I had to force the bow northward, holding and fighting the wheel.

Oh God, what if I snapped the rudder?

I pushed the throttle down a little harder just as a wave threatened us, and we surged up the wall of it, sprays of water—be they rain or ocean, I couldn't tell—pummelled me from the east. Not just water. Every self-doubt, every uncertainty swept over me, drenching me to the bone, and a cold, cold realisation that I was way out of my depth here, a sinking feeling of *what have I done* dropped on me from the clouds above.

It was different from any anxiety I'd experienced before. There were no walls closing in on me, there was no pressure on my chest, there was no struggle to breathe.

This wasn't a storm of my own doing.

I couldn't negotiate my way out of this. I couldn't sweet-talk or bluff; there was no deal to be made; there was nothing. I couldn't hold my stare across a boardroom desk and wait for the other man to fold first.

I had to hold my nerve as we went up a swell sideways, and I had to hold onto hope as the crest of a wave threatened to crash over us. Only the white tip was visible in the rain-soaked sky to my right.

But it didn't crash over us, it gave way underneath us, and we swung with the weight of gravity into the water, only to surge up again as the next swell rose.

I wondered if I could be too scared to be seasick.

I steered and backed off the speed as we lulled low in the valley of a wave, then sped up the oncoming wall of the next. And I'd been so busy watching the water on my right that I forgot to keep an eye on the island on the left until with the next flash of lightning, I realised it wasn't there.

Fuck!

Had I oversteered? Was I heading too far east? Into the reef, or worse still, had I taken us off the continental shelf into open water?

Panic struck me hard like a blow between the ribs, and I swung us port side. I gave no thought to timing or to the oncoming wave, and I thought for one heart-stopping second we were about to nosedive into the water. Whether it was the right thing to do, or the keel, or just good luck, the yacht righted and we lifted on the water. A discernible rise again, then we glided, smoother, with the wind and water, and pushed west.

Lightning boomed above, sheeting across the horizon, showing the sky was darkened, stormy. The rain was a deluge, just sheets of water. I had the feeling of being turned around so many times, I didn't know which direction was which.

I couldn't leave the wheel to check the navigation tablet. God, would it even work? Given how wet the entire deck and cockpit was?

The rain was now at my back, and the wind and water took us, so we must have been heading west. Or west enough, I guessed. And how long could we do that until we ran into something? The island, a reef? Coral could rip a hole through the hull, and in a flurry of panic that was becoming something close to abject terror, I began to swing the wheel to take us starboard.

And then lightning lit the sky again, and I saw it.

Some distance, maybe sixty metres away to the port

side, barely visible in the grey squall of the storm, was the sway and slant of palm trees.

The island.

I'd reached the top of the island.

I turned us inward, closer to shore, and with the rain and wind at my back, I knew I was still heading due west. No longer fighting the waves, we were flying in the wind. I had no idea how close the inlet was, but I veered us further inward, and the waves tried to correct my course, but I needed to turn, turn, turn. I needed to go *into* the inlet, not past it. The wind blew hard, the swell tried to dump us, and just as we rounded out of the squall, into the protection of this small harbour, we jolted, jerking in the water, yanking like a toy boat on a string.

Had I run us aground? Had I hit coral? Had I hit anything at all? Or was this just what yachts did? Did I turn too fast?

Then, like someone flipped a switch, without force, without fury, we glided along gentler waters. The rain still pelted and the wind roared above us, but the water was nowhere near as rough.

Back at the wheel, I slowed the throttle and killed the engine. The rain still fell, and the wind roared through the trees, and it was choppy, but nothing like what we'd just been through. We were protected here.

Against all the odds, against everything mother nature threw at me, I'd done it.

I'd got us to the inlet.

God knew what damage I'd done to the yacht, and I was sure Foster would kill me when he was feeling better... Shit! Foster. I dropped the anchor again, this time until it hit the sandy bottom, yanked the door open, and almost fell down the stairs. I closed the door behind me and the silence was almost deafening.

No wind, no rain, no water.

I ran straight to the bathroom and opened the door. Foster was still on the floor, around the other side of the toilet, his back to the seat cushion I'd put there. Whether he moved there of his volition or if he'd crashed and slid there with the rough sailing, I had no way of knowing. I knelt beside him and touched his face. He was still warm, and a bit of colour had returned, but his eyes fluttered open from sleep. He took a second to focus on me, then the slightest smile tugged at the corner of his mouth.

"Hey," I said, suddenly emotional. "You okay?"

"Tired," he mumbled. He closed his eyes again and didn't open them. Sleep was good. It meant he was getting better.

I stood up and covered him again with the sheet and came back with the opened bottle of Lucozade. I made him have a few sips. Though he protested at first, I explained he needed to replace his electrolytes and it would make him better. He sipped what he could, then soon passed out again.

Figuring he was best left where he was, I walked out and closed the door behind me. Standing in the middle of the cabin, water pooling around my feet, the adrenaline I'd been running on crashed all around me, and the reality of what I'd done seeped into me. I gripped the table, let my head fall forward, and cried.

CHAPTER SIXTEEN

FOSTER

I WOKE up on the bathroom floor and noticed two things. My body hurt, all over. Like I'd been hit by a truck. And I was wearing a floatation belt and nothing else. A floatation belt?

Slowly, recognition came back to me.

Sex, Stuart, laughing, eating... oysters.

My stomach rolled again, though I didn't vomit. I didn't think I could.

Then I remembered. Vomiting and vomiting, being sick and feeling like death warmed over. Worse than death. I remembered wishing for death. I would have welcomed it.

I sat up, every muscle protesting. My stomach and ribs hurt in the way they hurt after being violently ill for hours. My back and hips hurt, most likely from sleeping on the floor.

There was a half a bottle of Lucozade on the floor next to me, cushions from the table seat all around the floor.

What the hell?

Then I remembered Stuart wiping my face, asking if I felt okay, his look of true concern.

Stuart.

I got to my feet, feeling a little seedy and very sore but otherwise okay. I'd definitely felt better, but I'd survive. I wrapped a towel around my waist, opened the door, and looked into his cabin. The bed was unmade but empty, so I quickly pulled on some shorts, then found the lounge and galley were empty too. Things looked a little strewn, but my first concern was Stuart.

Where was he?

The door to the cockpit was shut, so I opened it and went up the stairs. The sky was blue, water was calm, and from where the sun sat barely over the horizon, I'd guess it was barely half six in the morning. There was no Stuart though... and then I noticed the island.

We weren't where we were supposed to be.

The last thing I remember was being on the east side of the island. When we went to my cabin yesterday, we were definitely on the east side of the island, away from people and prying eyes. We'd spent hours in bed, but we were definitely on the east side of Low Island, and now we were in the inlet?

What the...?

"Stuart?" I called out. He wasn't swimming off the back of the yacht. The ladder wasn't down. "Stuart!" With my heart in my throat, I raced below deck and threw open the two closed cabin doors, and there he was... in my bed.

Words would never describe the relief I felt.

He sat up, bleary-eyed, and tried to get up off the bed. "What's wrong? Is Foster okay?" Then he blinked and stopped, one foot on the floor. He saw me and sagged. "Oh. Hey."

"Hey," I replied. Then I noticed the floatation belt on the floor, the pile of wet towels beside it. "What happened?"

"You got food poisoning," he said, sitting back on the bed, scrubbing both hands over his face, then knuckled his eyes before giving me a tired smile. "But you look much better. What time is it? How do you feel?"

"I feel... I don't know how I feel. I meant, what happened? Why are we in the inlet?"

"There was a storm," he said, frowning. "It was bad. I didn't know what else to do, and I remembered you said the inlet would be safer."

"So you sailed? My yacht?" I felt nauseous again; that had nothing to do with eating bad seafood.

"You were on the floor," he said, a hurt look on his face. "A shade of green no person should be. I was fucking stressed and scared, and I didn't know what else to do!" He shot out of bed and went to walk past me.

I grabbed his arm. "Stop. I'm not mad."

He turned to look at me, but the defensive set of his jaw hadn't lessened at all.

"I'm shocked," I admitted. "And sorry. I can't believe you did that."

He pulled his arm free. "I didn't have much choice. It was either that or the rescue helicopter—"

"The rescue helicopter?" I was sure my eyes almost bugged out of my head.

"You were green. On the floor. There was a huge storm, and I thought we were going to capsize. They radioed for you. I didn't call them. I didn't even know how to speak with all the *over this, over that* bullshit."

He obviously thought I was still pissed at him, but I was just trying to get my head around it all. I put my hand on his shoulder. "Hey. You sailed!"

Eventually he smiled, the tension between us easing. "And I put the belt on you in case we went overboard."

I slid my hand down his arm to his fingers and gave them a squeeze. I hadn't missed what he said before, I was just trying to catch up. "You were scared."

"Petrified."

"I'm so sorry."

"It wasn't your fault," he whispered.

We both knew that wasn't true. I was responsible for his well-being out here, and I'd failed. Epically.

A wave of weariness dropped over me, and my stomach twisted with nausea, real nausea this time. "I need to sit down," I said. I undid the belt, and pulled it off.

"Go shower," he suggested. "It'll make you feel better. I'll make you some black tea."

"Will you tell me everything then?" I asked.

He nodded. "I think we can expect a visit from the Coast Guard boat. At least, they said they'd call around last night when I told them I'd made it to the inlet."

I nodded. "I'm really sorry you had to go through that alone."

He gave me a smile that didn't sit right on his face. "Go shower. I'll put the kettle on. Then you can go over your boat to see what damage I did to it."

"Damage?"

He shrugged and turned to the sink, busying himself with the kettle.

HE WAS RIGHT about the shower. It made me feel so much better. Human, almost. But he was wrong about the damage. There was none. Everything was perfect. Better than perfect. He'd probably prevented damage by sailing us around the island.

He stood on the deck, staring at the trees, a little perplexed. "What's wrong?" I asked.

"How can there be no damage? I was expecting trees down or stripped bare."

I rubbed his arm. "They suffer cyclones out here and bounce right back."

He afforded me a small smile. "And the boat?"

"She's perfect. Thank you."

"What are you thanking me for?"

"For saving my yacht. For saving us. For looking after me. For being as scared as hell but being brave enough to do it anyway."

"I just did what anyone would do," he mumbled.

"No, you did what few people could do. Stuart." I waited for him to look at me. "I can't remember much about last night. None of the storm. But I do seem to remember being sick as hell and seeing your face, taking care of me, wiping my face, making me drink." I gave him a smile. "Thank you. Not many people would have done that either."

"I was worried for you," he said gently. Then his eyes met mine, and that rare vulnerability was back. "I was shit scared."

I slid my hand around his neck and pulled him against me. "You did real good, Stu. And you know what?" I pulled back and held his arm so he had to look at me. "You said before you weren't brave enough to change your life. Well, you just proved that you are."

He made a face with a look in his eyes I couldn't quite identify. Then he seemed to change tack. "Can I ask you something?"

"Of course."

"White Knight, the name of your yacht..." He almost

smiled. "I didn't give it much thought, but the Coast Guard guy kept repeating it. I get that it's your name, but does it mean what I think it does?"

I smiled. "If you're thinking it means a friendly corporate takeover that outbids the hostile takeover of a black knight, you'd be correct."

He nodded slowly. "I thought so."

"My days of corporate hostility are over. It seemed fitting."

"It is." He swallowed hard, then asked, "How are you feeling?"

"Not great. But better than I was. With thanks to you." I took his hand and threaded our fingers. It was somehow, despite all the sex and kissing we'd done, one of our most intimate moments. "I better put a call through to the Coast Guard."

He nodded. "Yeah. And apologise for my lack of knowledge on protocol."

"Were they really gonna come out?"

He shrugged and made a thoughtful face. "Think so. How'd they know where we were anyway?"

"Live tracking. I'm registered, and they were probably just giving me a cautionary call, seeing the storm coming and our beacon not moving."

He sighed. "Well, I'm glad. Kinda felt very alone out here last night." He looked out across the picturesque island, calm and beautiful as it was. "I can't believe it's the same place."

I lifted his hand to my lips and kissed first his knuckles, then the palm of a hand. "Thank you. For everything you did. I always knew you were listening when I was telling you how to sail and what to do, but I didn't think you'd need it."

"Neither did I."

There was a quietness to him, and I was unsure of the cause of it. Was he still shaken from last night? Or was he angry? Did he think me irresponsible? Did he want to leave? "So," I hedged. "Still got one more day. Did you want to head back to Cairns early?"

He frowned. "Why? Are you still feeling sick?"

"No, I just thought you might have had enough excitement for one day to last you a while."

"To last me forever," he added. But then he took in a deep breath and gave me half a smile. "I don't want to go back early."

I don't want to go back at all followed in my mind, and I hoped he'd say it. But there was only silence. Was he on the same page? Did he feel what I felt? Before I could ask, he pulled on my hand and led me to the stairs.

"Come on. Let's get you that tea, and you can call the Coast Guard before they come looking for us."

THE CALL to the Coast Guard was brief but informative. It was a Category 2 storm, not super dangerous by any means, but Stuart had navigated and sailed, by himself, in the dark, alone. Driving rain, blowing winds, high swells. I don't think he realised the extent of his actions. Would we have been in any danger if he'd not sailed us into the protected inlet? Impossible to tell, but it was likely.

He'd done the right thing. He'd done a brave thing.

"Oh," I spoke into the mouthpiece. "Mr Jenner sends his apologies for not knowing radio protocol. Over."

The Coast Guard's response was a happy sound. "Make

sure you teach him if he's gonna be sailing some more. And tell him he did real good. Over."

I smiled at Stuart, who was sitting at the table and hearing the entire conversation. "I will. Over and out."

I hung the two-way receiver in its cradle and went to him. He'd made black tea and a piece of plain toast. "Did you want to try and eat?"

My stomach rolled and I shook my head. "Not yet. I'll take the tea, though."

Things were quiet between us, not entirely in a good way, but not in a bad way either. It was like things needed to be said, the air needed to be cleared. "I owe you a lot," I started. "For last night. For looking after me and sailing out of the storm. That really did take guts. I know you're not good with personal compliments, but I'm really proud of you."

He blushed, and although he didn't say anything in response, he gave the smallest of smiles. Then, in typical Stuart form, he changed the subject. "So, I have one more day. One more night..."

I sipped my tea and waited to see how my stomach would react. "What did you want to do?"

"I want to do nothing," he replied in almost a whisper. "I want to sit up on deck and not miss a minute of the view, the sun."

He didn't want to miss a minute today because he was leaving tomorrow. And suddenly the tea was a bad idea. I pushed it away and tried to smile for him. "Then that's what we'll do."

"With you," he added, meeting my eyes. "I want to sit with you. And not miss a minute *with you*."

My heart banged against my ribs. "I want that too."

He smiled sadly, then brightened as if he had to make himself. "Then I'll go get changed. The white Speedos it is."

I laughed despite feeling under the weather and heavy-hearted.

While he changed and went up to the deck, I cleaned the bathroom and disinfected what I could. Cleaning where I'd been ill made me feel a bit better, so I took some crackers and a fresh bottle of Lucozade, and when I found him upstairs, he was sprawled face down on a towel, sunning himself to a golden bronze.

"Wondered where you were," he mumbled, his eyes still closed.

I sat beside him, then lay on my side so I could study his face. "You're really beautiful," I said, as gentle as the breeze.

His lips curled into a smile; his eyelids opened slowly. "As are you."

"You've seen me at my worst," I said. "Last night, violently ill. While stark naked. Hardly beautiful."

He snorted out a laugh and rolled onto his side, our bodies, our faces, just a few inches apart. He trailed his fingers through the hair at my temple. "Do you feel better?"

I nodded. "A little. Not sure I'll be up for any last-day sex marathons though. Sorry."

He searched my eyes and eventually said, "I don't mind. I just want this. To be here with you, like this."

And that is exactly how we stayed. He rolled into me, shuffling until he could use my arm as his pillow, and he snoozed. Given he'd had such an awful night, I doubted he'd slept much, so I didn't mind at all. It gave me time to relish the quiet, the unspoken, the closeness. Him in my arms in the warmth of the sun.

Then later when the sun became too hot, we swam in the

cool water of the inlet. I only went in briefly, but I sat at the edge of the deck with my feet in the water and watched him. After that, we sat on the bench seat in the cockpit with me leaning against the end and him between my legs, his back to my chest, so I could kiss the top of his head, hold him in my arms.

And that was how we spent his last full day. Always touching, always close.

Unfortunately, we had to go back to the mainland before sunset. The plan would be to stay up near Port Douglas, then head down to Cairns in the morning. I asked him if he wanted to be the one to sail back to the coast, but he quickly declined. He sat with me while I manned the wheel, his hand on my leg instead.

Our original plan had been to tuck in between Wentworth Reef and Port Douglas, and we could dock if he wanted to go to a restaurant on the mainland. But he didn't want to. He didn't want to get off the yacht.

He had to feel the same as me. He had to. He needed to touch me, to be near me, like he knew our time was almost over and he could barely stand it. Even if he couldn't say it, his actions spoke the loudest.

By dinner time, I could stomach dry toast and tea, which we ate in the cockpit. There were other boats around, not too close, but Stuart didn't seem to mind now. He didn't even seem to notice. He simply planted himself back in my arms and we watched the sunset over the water.

Our last one.

Our last night.

And even as darkness fell, neither of us moved. "I don't want this to end," I whispered, followed by a kiss above his ear.

"Me either," he replied, making my blood sing and my heart thump.

Surely he had to hear it hammering in my chest...

"Let's go to bed," he murmured, getting to his feet and pulling me up by the hand. We closed up the cabin and went into his room, where he stripped out of his Speedos. His cock was full, and although my body reacted, I just wasn't sure I could. "Stuart, I..."

He smiled as he slid into bed naked. "We don't have to do anything," he said, patting the bed beside him. "I just want to be with you."

I stripped off and turned off the lights, then joined him in bed. He slid into my side, the way magnets do, with his head in the crook of my arm.

I wanted to tell him to stay. I wanted to tell him to quit his job, his old life, and stay with me.

I wanted to tell him how I felt.

But as I searched for the right words, his breathing evened out and he slept. I drew him in close and wrapped my arms around him, and even though he couldn't hear me, or maybe because he couldn't hear me, I said the words anyway. "I'm falling in love with you."

———

I WOKE up feeling so much better. And I woke up with Stuart's arse pressed hard against my cock. Maybe that was the reason I felt so good, but either way, it was an extremely pleasant way of waking up.

The sky was barely light outside, so I knew it was early, and I ran my hand up over his hip. "Morning," he murmured, still sleepy.

I kissed the back of his head and my spine curled involuntarily, pressing my hips hard and hot against him. "Morning."

Then I remembered it was his last day, and I froze.

"I leave today," he whispered like he knew where my mind had gone.

I kissed his shoulder. "I know."

He pushed his arse back. "One last time," he said gruffly. "Please."

A shudder coursed through me, and he groaned low in his throat.

"Stay right here," I replied. I rolled over to the bedside, quickly finding what I needed. I got myself ready, then him. Slick fingers found his hole and he arched onto me.

"No," he whined. "I need you. Inside me. Just do it."

"You're not ready," I replied, but he lifted his leg, reached behind to grab my cock, and guided me inside him.

I breached him slowly, and he arched his back, giving me better access, and I slid in. "Oh fuck, Stuart," I breathed, trying to stem the urgency, the desire to ram into him.

I gripped his hip and gently bit his shoulder, and he cried out, arching some more. "Foster, please. I want to feel it for days. Make me feel it for days."

Oh fuck.

So I gripped a little harder and pushed in deeper. He moaned, long and low, and he began to stroke himself.

"Move in me," he begged. "Fuck me."

So I did.

I pushed him onto his stomach, rolling on top of him, and before he could complain, I rammed into him. Just how he liked it. Just how he needed it.

I drew out a little and pushed in deeper, all the way. He gripped the sheets, crying out as I buried my entire length inside him. But he lifted his arse and he moved his hips and I ploughed into him again.

I slid my arms under his chest and held onto him as I

gave him exactly what he wanted. Then I stopped, letting him savour the feeling of being owned, and I kissed the back of his neck to tell him not to leave me. And I thrust in deep, nipping the skin of his shoulder to beg him to stay.

And he came in response, shuddering underneath me, squeezing my cock and milking my orgasm from my bones, my soul. I came so hard, holding him, buried so deep inside him.

But I couldn't find the words. Speech escaped me, fear engulfed me. And everything I wanted to say went unsaid.

WE SAILED DOWN THE COAST, meandering on a slow wind and avoiding a conversation we needed to have. A conversation neither one of us were keen to start. He disappeared below deck while I concentrated on sailing, and it gave me time to mentally prepare the words I needed to say.

When he came up the stairs, his steps slow, I knew this was it. I met his gaze and took a deep breath, ready to put my heart on the line.

"I'm packed," he said.

I blinked. "You're what?"

"I'm all packed up. Ready to go." He let out a slow breath. "My flight's at twelve."

My hand fell from the wheel and I stared, stupefied. "Or not."

"What?"

My heart was in my throat and I could barely swallow around it. "Or you could not go." My speech wasn't going to plan. Visions in my head of me giving him some romantic spiel about following his heart and choosing me were going horribly wrong. "You could stay."

He gave me a sad smile. "I can't."

"Why not?"

He ran his hand through his hair and looked out to sea. "I have a life there. I can't just walk away."

"Yes you can. You're not happy there. You said so. You said you wanted to stay here. With me."

"I said I *wish* I could." His sad smile turned to one of pity. "But it was just a silly dream. It wasn't real."

Those words stung like he'd slapped me. "It was real for me."

"Foster," he started, reaching for me.

I pulled my arm away. "Forget it. I didn't realise none of this was real for you. I should have, and I was an idiot. Sorry."

"Foster, that's not what I meant—"

"I think it's pretty clear what you meant." I looked to the bow of the yacht and raised my chin. This conversation was done. I was done. I'd foolishly let my guard down, and look where it got me.

"I just—"

"We'll be coming into port soon," I spoke over him.

He was a smart man; he took the hint. He sat on the bench seat, not close to me like he usually did, and he pulled his phone from his pocket. He switched it on, and in the seconds that followed, the beeps started. And they didn't stop.

Messages. Emails. Missed calls.

His shoulders sagged more and more with every sound. He just sat there and stared at the screen as the phone continued to beep, and then it actually rang. But he didn't answer it. He just sat there and stared at it.

And a glimmer of hope took hold in my chest.

He didn't want that life. He hated it, and it was killing him. Like it had almost killed me.

"You gonna answer that?" I asked over the ringing phone.

His gaze met mine and his eyes shone like he was fighting tears. But there was an edge to his jaw and his nostrils flared, and he shot up from his seat and was gone, down the stairs, before I could blink.

"Stuart," I called out, but a cabin door slamming was his only reply.

I couldn't leave the wheel. We were coming into port, there was a lot of traffic, and I needed to be at the helm. And I tried to see reason, and I tried to see things from his perspective. I'd been in his shoes, after all. I knew *exactly* what he was going through.

But I just got more pissed off the closer to port we got.

I knew exactly what kind of person it took to do the job he did, and it took stubbornness, ego, and defiance. And I had all three in spades. If he thought he could out-manoeuvre me, he was wrong.

If he wanted to be gone, then so be it. I pulled the main-sail in, kicked over the engine, and sailed into the harbour.

It was busy, as always, and that pissed me off too.

There were boats, cruisers, businesses, all going about their days like nothing was wrong. On land, there were people about without a care in the world, walking, some jogging, some strolling along with dogs or pushing prams. Palm trees swayed like my world wasn't ending.

Like my heart wasn't breaking.

I moored the yacht and waited for him to come up. If he was getting off this boat, he could damn well look me in the eye as he did it.

Eventually, after what felt like forever, he came into the cockpit, dressed in proper shorts and a shirt, duffle bag in hand. *My God, he's really leaving.*

I didn't even try to hide the anger in my voice. "I didn't think you'd fold."

"Fold?"

"Like a pack of fucking cards. I thought you were a man of integrity who believed in himself and could make ballsy decisions and stand his ground. But apparently I was wrong."

Instant anger flared in his eyes, and he pointed his finger at me. "You don't get to judge me. You don't get to say what's right for me. I have an entire life back in Brisbane. People who depend on me."

"Bullshit. You have a boss that would replace you before the ink on your resignation letter was dry. You have guys that you meet with to scratch a physical itch. If it's not you they get it with, they'll just find someone else. Just like you would."

His nostrils flared. "Just like I *did*, you mean?"

"What we had was more than that, and you know it."

He threw his hands up, frustration winning out. "What do you want me to say? That I'll quit my job and move up here to be with you? Do you think we'd get some fairy tale ending, sail off into the sunset together? This isn't a fucking Disney movie, Foster."

"I'm acutely aware of that, Stuart. And I never expected you to want me. I'm not fucking blind. You're a young hotshot financier, and I'm a washed-up guy who couldn't hack it. So no, I never expected you to want me, but I did expect you to make a stand."

"A stand for what?" he cried.

God, is he fucking blind? "For the life you want. Not the

life you feel obliged to live. You only get one life, and you're not happy in yours. Make the change. Quit. You don't have to move up here, though I'd love it if you did. Just do whatever makes you happy."

He stared for the longest time. His phone beeped, message after message, and when it rang, he looked at the screen. "Fuck!" he growled in frustration. "I need to take this."

"Yeah, okay. I get it," I mumbled, the fight in me gone. My entire mental speech had gone so very wrong, but in the end, it didn't matter. It was over. He was going to leave, and I was going to let him. I couldn't very well make him stay.

He answered the call. "Stuart Jenner... Yes, certainly. Can you just hold on for one second and you'll have my undivided attention... Thanks." He put the phone to his chest and held out his hand for me to shake. "Foster, I need to go."

Shaking hands? After everything we'd done together?

I didn't think so.

I looked at his hand, not even trying to hide how offended I was. His face fell and he lowered his hand. "I was never any good at goodbyes," he whispered.

I wanted to hold him. I wanted to crush him against me, feel every hill and valley of his body against mine, where he fit so right. I wanted to kiss him one more time... But instead, I took a step back and made it easy for him.

He gave a nod. "Foster... Thank you for everything. I had the best two weeks... of my life. I'll never forget..." He swallowed hard. "Thank you. I'm sorry I couldn't be what you thought..."

I nodded back, determined not to let my emotions show. "Goodbye, Stuart."

He collected his bag and put the phone back to his ear

as he walked off the jetty. I stood there in the blistering sun and warm tropical winds feeling cold and heavy. I watched him get into a taxi, and I watched him drive away, his phone still to his ear. He didn't look back. He didn't even wave.

So that was really it.

He was gone.

I WENT BACK on board my yacht, completed an all-systems check, filled in logbooks, then stripped the beds, emptied bins, cleaned and sterilised everything. Like I always did after every job. Mechanically. Without feeling. Numb.

Then I set about getting it ready for the next lot of clients, due to arrive in two days. Apparently, I had two couples from Japan booked in for a three-day cruise. Just a short one this time, not two weeks. I made a mental note to tell the head office I'd rather not do long jobs any more. Nothing over a week, I decided. And never with one client.

It was too personal, too intimate.

I was too invested.

I received the particulars list from the head office for the next job, including food requirements, and I put a grocery order in to be delivered first thing in the morning of our departure.

I'd had crazy visions of Stuart turning up on the jetty, running in like some stupid movie, telling me he couldn't board the plane. Telling me he couldn't leave; he wanted to be with me.

But he didn't.

And as my work was all done and the sun set, the sky grew dark, I knew he was really gone.

I was really alone.

Despite the noise of the harbour, the noise of the marina, the voices, the birds, I'd never felt more alone. I took the bottle of tequila and sat at my dining table. Before Stuart, I'd relished the silence. Now it was the last thing I wanted.

I poured myself a shot, but it didn't taste the same.

I needed to lick salt off his skin, to bite lemon from his mouth for it to ever taste the same again.

When my phone buzzed with a text message, my heart leapt. Was it him? Did he stay?

I saw his name and butterflies flooded my stomach.

I'm home. I wish I wasn't.

I'm leaving for Sydney in the morning. I wish I wasn't.

I'm sorry for how things ended.

I wish I was as brave as you.

I could be the real me with you, for the first time in my life.

I will never forget you.

Every time I see a sunset or a sunrise, I'll think of you. A beach, a boat, a bottle of tequila. People in love.

I will think of you.

MY HEART SQUEEZED to the point of pain. Angry tears, heartbroken tears filled my eyes, and I threw my phone at the fucking wall.

Fuck him.

Fuck him for coming here, for making me realise what I'm missing. But most of all, fuck him for leaving.

I wouldn't reply. I couldn't. It didn't change anything.

TWO DAYS LATER, I met my new clients on the jetty in the harbour, like I always did. They were very nice, very polite, always nodding at me, always smiling.

But they didn't challenge me, not like Stuart. They didn't pick up after themselves, not like Stuart. They didn't talk to me for hours, they didn't make me laugh, they didn't make me feel anything, not like Stuart.

The sunset didn't look the same.

The sunrise didn't have the same endless-possibility feel.

My yacht, my home wasn't the same.

The sun, the wind, the ocean weren't the same.

Then it struck me with the clarity of a squeeze of my heart, that it wasn't true. Everything was exactly the same. Everything was as it should be. The thing that was different was me.

CHAPTER SEVENTEEN

STUART

I HATED SYDNEY. I didn't belong here, and the likelihood of me moving here was a heavy lump in my gut. I didn't want to be here. Not for these two weeks, not for this merger, not for anything.

The grey and gloomy city through rain-splattered windows empathised with my mood.

I didn't want to be here.

I wanted to be thousands of kilometres away on a white yacht surrounded by miles of blue. Blue water, blue skies, blue eyes...

This Sydney deal was big, and I'd been here as an analyst with Paulington, with my boss Gerard Soto, for two weeks finalising the details. Bull & Keo was the biggest fish in the corporate pond, and they wanted me to stay. They made no attempt at hiding it, jokingly telling Gerard I could do better with them. They wined and dined me, under the pretence of business with Paulington, though trying to entice me to their side of a very lucrative line.

They offered me a shitload of money, and they offered me a choice of locations. Sydney, Singapore, Jakarta. I could take my pick, be a part of their global team and conquer the world.

It didn't get any bigger than this.

It was everything I'd worked my arse off for. It was an offer other people would kill for, and I should have grabbed it with both hands. I shouldn't have hesitated. I shouldn't have told them I'd need time to consider their offer.

My brain was telling me *take it, take it, take it*. My heart was yearning for something else.

Someone else.

Someone else who hadn't replied to my text. Someone else who had told me I was gutless, who had let me walk away.

I'd sent other texts...

I'm sorry.

I was wrong.

If I could just stand on that jetty one more time...

He didn't reply to any of them. Of course he hadn't. He'd been brave enough to say it to my face.

I stared out the window, heavy-hearted and lost, not interested in the deal that was now done, the way people shook hands and offered congratulations, clapped each other on the back and smiled.

"Well done, Mr Jenner," I was told. I was cheered, thanked, congratulated in a mindless haze, and was whisked down to the King Street Wharf, to a fine-dining restaurant on Darling Harbour. I was surrounded by Italian suits, French champagne, and Cuban cigars, in the midst of hollow conversations and empty promises. As we were seated at the long table to fit all twelve of us, the wealth and power surrounding me were staggering. The men at this table influenced economies.

A bubble of panic began to expand in my chest.

A hand clapped my arm. "Get used to the accolades, Mr Jenner. When you work for us, this will be your new normal."

Fucking hell.

I didn't want this.

I didn't want exotic countries, extraordinary opportunities, expensive suits in executive apartments. I didn't want any of it.

I looked out across the harbour, at the cruise ships, the water taxis, the yachts...

A fresh glass of champagne was put in my hand, and I couldn't even speak. I was about to have a full-on panic attack in front of everyone. My lungs squeezed. My heart beat out of rhythm.

"Mr Jenner? Everything okay?"

I looked at the concerned faces at the table.

Breathe, Stuart.

But I couldn't quite seem to manage it, and the bubble of panic expanded a little more. I was losing it. I needed fresh air and...

What did Foster say? There would be a moment and I would know. My tipping point moment—when I knew I would leave—would be crystal clear and pointedly sharp. In that moment, you'll know, he'd said. Because if you don't walk out, you'll die.

Jesus. He was right.

I tried to breathe but couldn't quite manage it. My chest felt tight, my ribs too small.

"Excuse me, Mr Jenner," a waiter interrupted. "This is for you, with the message, 'Looks like you could use a shot.'"

He slid a bottle of Alquimia Reserva de Don Adolfo Extra Añejo tequila in front of me.

Foster's tequila.

I shot my gaze to the waiter. "What? Who...?"

"At the bar," he replied with a polite smile.

I didn't even realise I was on my feet until I craned my neck, looking, searching...

And there he was. Sitting at a table, leaning back like he owned the place, wearing cargo shorts and a polo shirt, his leather deck shoes, and a shit-eating grin.

Foster.

I almost cried with relief. My eyes burned. My heart sang.

I'd never wanted anything more.

In that second, that moment, everything was crystal clear.

I wanted to go to him, to crawl into his arms, and never leave, but I couldn't seem to move. Like he somehow knew I was stuck, he shot to his feet and casually walked over. He was so incredibly underdressed, yet with the confidence he exuded, he could have very well owned this place and everyone in it.

He walked to the table, glancing around at the faces looking back at him. "Gentlemen." Then he nodded to some in particular. "Jack. Carlos. Larry." They stared at him like they couldn't place his face in those casual clothes. I guessed they were only used to seeing him wearing sharp tailored suits.

Then Foster bowed his head. "Mr Shimizu. Always an honour."

The small Japanese man obviously recognised him immediately because he stood and bowed as well. "Mr Knight. What brings you here? I thought you were no longer active." As soon as Mr Shimizu said his name, quiet gasps went around the table and heads whipped around in his direction.

Foster grinned. "I'm just here to do what white knights do best."

"And what's that?" Larry Sterling asked from the head of the table. He didn't look particularly pleased.

Foster smirked at him. "A friendly takeover bid that outbids the black knight. I don't believe a hostile takeover is necessary here."

Sterling barked out a laugh, and it might have worked if not for the hint of fear in his eyes. "And pray tell, Knight. Just which company do you intend to make a bid for?"

"I don't want any company," Foster replied smoothly. He looked right at me. "I'm here for something a little more personal."

I let out a laugh, and my lungs burned and my eyes watered like I'd been held underwater and had just broke the surface.

Foster stared right at me. "What do you reckon? Want to sail around the Whitsundays with me? Forever?"

I answered with a quick nod. "God, yes."

He grinned. "I'm double-parked," he said, nodding toward the harbour. I looked outside and could see a crowd gathered on the wharf around his yacht despite the drizzling rain, marvelling at its beauty.

I grinned at him, every cell in my body buzzing.

"You ready?" he asked.

I nodded. "So ready." I looked at all the faces staring at me, some confused, some furious. "Thank you, gentlemen," I said. "It's been great and all, but I would like to respectfully decline your invitation to join your team. I've had a better offer."

I grabbed the bottle of tequila, gave them a parting nod, and when Foster held out his hand, I took it. The warmth, the strength, the familiar touch filled me with something new, something exciting, something right. And together, hand in hand, we ran out of the restaurant, into the rain, across the wharf, and stepped onto his yacht.

His home.

"Get the moor lines," he said as he kicked the engine over.

I bent at the back and wound in the lines, tying them off like he'd showed me. I stepped down in the cockpit, grinning. Foster's smile matched mine as he stood at the wheel, steering us away from the wharf. I slid my arms around him and tucked myself into his side.

"I can't believe you're here," I whispered.

"It took me seven days to sail here," he said, looking over the bow, navigating the harbour.

Seven days? "Why didn't you let me know you were coming?"

"Once I decided I was coming for you, I didn't stop. I dropped my last clients back at base and couldn't stand the silence one more second. Not one more second without you," he said. With one hand on the wheel, he kissed me then. I clung to him, savouring his lips, his tongue, his touch. With a hum, he drew back and looked ahead again as we continued to sail, but he smiled. "I called your office to find where you were, expecting Brisbane. They said you were in Sydney, so I figured I was halfway here. Anyway, was my entrance back there not exciting? Romantic?"

I snorted and held him a little tighter. "I've never been so grateful to see anyone."

"You looked like you could use a little bit of help back there."

"I was drowning," I murmured into his neck. "That was my tipping point back there. My leave or die moment."

"I know," he said with a smile, still looking ahead, but

his arm around me tightened. "There were some pretty big names at that table."

"I didn't want that life. I didn't want any of it."

"I know."

"Every second since I left you felt like the world was closing in on me." I looked up at him, at his square jaw, his eyes. "You saved me back there."

He kissed me again, pushing me against the wheel, and before we could get carried away, he pulled back with a groan. "We won't make it out of the harbour at this rate."

"Then drop anchor," I suggested.

"We have to be back in Cairns harbour in eight days." He licked his lips, almost nervous. "Are you sure you want this life?"

I met his gaze so he could see the honesty in mine. "Never been surer."

"What about your clothes, your bags at the hotel?" he asked like he'd just thought of them.

"Fuck it," I said. "I won't need any of it where we're going. And we've got eight days to figure out what to do with my apartment in Brisbane. And my car." There was so much to think about, but I really didn't care.

As we approached the heads out of Sydney, Foster had me raise the main. The seas were rough with high swells, but the stormy weather meant the wind was strong, and we were soon sailing, flying on the water, north to where we needed to be.

He laughed as I took my suit coat off and threw it on the cockpit floor. I toed out of my shoes and pulled my socks off, then pulled off my tie, undid the top two buttons of my shirt. I held my tie up in the wind, letting out a long "woooooooooo" into the wind as I stood with Foster at my side. We were wet from the drizzling rain but we were headed out of the storm, to brighter skies, calmer waters. To where the azure waters met white sands, to where the only thing better than seeing the sunset was watching it rise. Where the only thing hotter than the tropics was the man standing beside me.

EPILOGUE

STUART

THE SUN WAS BLISTERING, the wind was warm, the sound of the water lapping at the hull made me smile.

I was lying on the deck, wearing nothing but Speedos, and Foster was resting his head on my belly. I was almost snoozing and he, like he often did, was playing with an old piece of rope, tying and untying knots. He did it with his eyes closed, and I played with his hair.

It was five years ago this week that he'd sailed into Sydney harbour and whisked me away in a fairy-tale-like fashion that stole my heart.

Well, that's not true. He'd stolen it well before then.

I chuckled as I remembered the trip from Sydney to Cairns.

"What's funny?" he asked.

I toyed with his hair, teasing the strands between my fingers and stroking his scalp. "Remembering Nelson's Bay. How we only made it as far as that before we had to drop anchor."

He chuckled, a husky rumble. "I thought we did well to make it that far."

"My God, you made short work of me that day."

Now he laughed. "And you loved every minute of it."

"Every second." I hummed. "If I think about what you did to me, I can still feel it."

He shot me a humoured look. The rope stilled in his hand. "Want a reminder?"

"Hell, yes."

"God. Didn't you get enough of me this morning?"

I stroked his hair. "Never enough."

The sun was making us drowsy.

"Oh." I just remembered. "Aunty Kim called when you were in the shower earlier. Just wanted to say hi."

He hummed and closed his eyes. "I'll call her back later." He loved it when I played with his hair, and his peaceful, sleepy demeanour made me smile. "Did you want me to make dinner reservations back on the mainland?" he asked, his voice lazy.

"Nope." He knew what my answer would be before he even asked the question. I never wanted to go to shore when we were out here. Just us. I loved the bubble we surrounded ourselves in.

In the last five years, I'd done as he first suggested. I worked the stock market, made educated guesses at where the trends and lags would be, when to buy, when to sell. I was better at it than I ever was in mergers and acquisitions.

But I didn't live on the boat.

I sold my apartment in Brisbane and bought an older style beach house north of Cairns. In one fell swoop, I'd gone from living sleek and sophisticated—and being bloody miserable—to a guy who rarely wore shoes and lived in an old weather-beaten house that fronted the ocean with its very own jetty. Where I could keep one eye on the world economy and one eye on the Coral Sea, looking for a sleek white yacht with a handsome skipper at the helm. And I was, without any doubt, the happiest I'd ever been.

I worked when it suited me, and I helped Foster run his private charter business. If he was making a scheduled stop on the coast, I'd meet him at any marina he moored at. When he wasn't working, the yacht was moored and we were either at the house or on board locked away together in his cabin. But we were together two, three, sometimes four nights a week. I'd done a few jobs with him when he needed an extra pair of hands on deck, but for the most part, we worked separately. We were realists, above all else. There was no way we could work together on the yacht and live together on the yacht day in and day out and expect to last longer than a few months.

So, we worked separately, our lives otherwise intertwined at every point possible, and we were disgustingly happy.

This was our fifth anniversary, and we were taking three days to sail out to the reef and spend our time completely removed and uninterrupted. It was utterly remote and downright perfect.

"You know, I think I need a new pair of Speedos," I mused.

He stopped making a knot and glanced up at me. "Are you trying to get me to look at your dick?"

I snorted. "No. If I wanted you to look, I'd be naked right now."

He made a happy sound and went back to knot making, his eyes closed, going by feel. "As long as the new pair are white. And see-through when wet."

Yes. God forbid I bought any other colour. I bought a black pair once and he hated them.

I watched him work the rope through his fingers,

methodically practising, turning it into steadfast knots I couldn't replicate, even with YouTube video instructions.

"What knot are you making?" I asked.

He looked at the rope in his hands like he was only just now seeing it, then he lifted it toward me. I took it, trying to figure out how he manipulated the different strands of rope to look like they were one. "It's for you," he said.

"What's it called?" All knots had weird names, and I tried to learn them as he told me. This one was different, and it was so secure, it looked unbreakable.

He sat up and faced me, a strange look on his face. "It's for you."

I almost laughed, and I probably would have if it weren't for the look on his face. Like he was both uncertain and completely sure at the same time. I sat up, our knees bent and touching. "Is it called the 'it's for you' knot?"

He shook his head and laughed. "No. I made it for you. It's called the 'true love's knot' because once it's done, and done right, it stays like that forever."

I looked at how the rope was twisted, knotted, separate strands becoming one. "I can see that." Sure, it was impressive, but... "Why is it for me?"

"Because I want you to marry me."

My head jerked up, shocked. I'm sure my expression said it all. "What?"

"Marry me." He licked his lips and swallowed hard. "I could organise some underwater snorkelling proposal or a sky-writing proposal if you'd prefer. Something full of romance and fanfare. I could take you to Paris, but..." He looked around the ocean, at the expanse of nothing but vast water, infinite skies, and us. "But this is all I need right here. Just you and forever."

Oh my God, he was serious.

My brain short-circuited. My heart stopped beating, but I nodded. I held out the knot, the forever knot. And there, in the middle of the ocean, by the coral reef and with the islands in the distance, I was surrounded by all I'd ever need. Foster and the promise of forever. "Yes."

He tackle-kissed me until he was lying on top of me, smiling down at me. "I think we better take this down into the cabin."

I grinned up at him. "Will it be Foster Jenner-Knight? Or Foster Knight-Jenner."

He kissed me with smiling lips, took my hands, and pinned them to the deck above my head. "Do you want my surname?" he asked. His eyes grew dark. He clearly liked the idea of that, very much.

"Yes. And you can have mine."

He used his knees to spread my thighs, my hands kept tight above my head. His hips were flush with mine, his erection hard and pressing against me in all the right places. "Stuart Jenner-Knight," he whispered. "I love the sound of that."

I rolled my hips. "I can tell."

He groaned, but then his eyes searched mine. "You'll really marry me?" He let go of my hands so he could trace the side of my face.

I nodded. "Yes. I was yours for forever anyway, when you sailed into Darling Harbour and rescued me. But you made me a forever knot with an old piece of rope, so now it's official."

He smiled and planted a soft kiss on my lips. "I wasn't supposed to blurt it out like that. I probably could have planned it better. But it just felt right."

"It was perfect. I don't need Paris or any fancy

proposals in expensive restaurants or special fanfare. I just need you."

"And so you have me, mister Stuart Jenner-Knight. Forever."

"Yes. Forever. I have the knot to prove it."

He laughed and kissed me again, this time longer, with more purpose. "Excuse me, Mister Foster Jenner-Knight," I said breathily when he kissed down my jaw. "You better take me below deck and finish what you started."

His eyes gleamed; his smile was filthy and full of promise. "Well, I am the ship's captain," he said, jumping up and pulling me to my feet. "And all good captains need a willing cabin boy."

I stopped. "Can I still be a cabin boy if we're married?"

He laughed. "You can be my cabin boy forever."

"Even when we're old and grey?"

He grinned. "I'll be very disappointed if you're not."

"Me too," I replied. I picked up the knot he'd made for me, leaned up on my toes and kissed him. "Now hurry up. Your cabin boy's impatient and horny. Best not to keep him waiting."

He laughed as he followed me below deck. He pulled the door closed, blocking out the rest of the world behind us. "How many days have we got?" he asked, walking me backwards into his cabin.

I held up the knotted rope. "We don't have days. We have forever."

THE END

ABOUT THE AUTHOR

N.R. Walker is an Australian author, who loves her genre of gay romance. She loves writing and spends far too much time doing it, but wouldn't have it any other way.

She is many things: a mother, a wife, a sister, a writer. She has pretty, pretty boys who live in her head, who don't let her sleep at night unless she gives them life with words.

She likes it when they do dirty, dirty things... but likes it even more when they fall in love.

She used to think having people in her head talking to her was weird, until one day she happened across other writers who told her it was normal.

She's been writing ever since...

SPECIAL THANKS

A special thank you to Shira Anthony who helped with the sailing details. May your days sailing in retirement be plentiful, and the weather perfect.

You can find Shira's amazing books at:
shiraanthony.com

ALSO BY N.R. WALKER

Blind Faith

Through These Eyes (Blind Faith #2)

Blindside: Mark's Story (Blind Faith #3)

Ten in the Bin

Point of No Return – Turning Point #1

Breaking Point – Turning Point #2

Starting Point – Turning Point #3

Element of Retrofit – Thomas Elkin Series #1

Clarity of Lines – Thomas Elkin Series #2

Sense of Place – Thomas Elkin Series #3

Taxes and TARDIS

Three's Company

Red Dirt Heart

Red Dirt Heart 2

Red Dirt Heart 3

Red Dirt Heart 4

Red Dirt Christmas

Cronin's Key

Cronin's Key II

Cronin's Key III

Exchange of Hearts

The Spencer Cohen Series, Book One

The Spencer Cohen Series, Book Two

The Spencer Cohen Series, Book Three

The Spencer Cohen Series, Yanni's Story

Blood & Milk

The Weight Of It All

A Very Henry Christmas (The Weight of It All 1.5)

Perfect Catch

Switched

Imago

Imagines

Red Dirt Heart Imago

On Davis Row

Finders Keepers

Evolved

Galaxies and Oceans

Titles in Audio:

Cronin's Key

Cronin's Key II

Cronin's Key III

Red Dirt Heart

Red Dirt Heart 2

Red Dirt Heart 3

Red Dirt Heart 4

The Weight Of It All

Switched

Point of No Return

Breaking Point

Starting Point

Spencer Cohen Book One

Spencer Cohen Book Two

Spencer Cohen Book Three

Yanni's Story

On Davis Row

Free Reads:

Sixty Five Hours

Learning to Feel

His Grandfather's Watch (And The Story of Billy and Hale)

The Twelfth of Never (Blind Faith 3.5)

Twelve Days of Christmas (Sixty Five Hours Christmas)

Best of Both Worlds

Translated Titles:

Fiducia Cieca (Italian translation of Blind Faith)

Attraverso Questi Occhi (Italian translation of Through These Eyes)

Preso alla Sprovvista (Italian translation of Blindside)

Il giorno del Mai (Italian translation of Blind Faith 3.5)

Cuore di Terra Rossa (*Italian translation of Red Dirt Heart*)

Cuore di Terra Rossa 2 (*Italian translation of Red Dirt Heart 2*)

Cuore di Terra Rossa 3 (*Italian translation of Red Dirt Heart 3*)

Cuore di Terra Rossa 4 (*Italian translation of Red Dirt Heart 4*)

Intervento di Retrofit (*Italian translation of Elements of Retrofit*)

Confiance Aveugle (*French translation of Blind Faith*)

A travers ces yeux: Confiance Aveugle 2 (*French translation of Through These Eyes*)

Aveugle: Confiance Aveugle 3 (*French translation of Blindside*)

À Jamais (*French translation of Blind Faith 3.5*)

Cronin's Key (*French translation*)

Cronin's Key II (*French translation*)

Au Coeur de Sutton Station (*French translation of Red Dirt Heart*)

Partir ou rester (*French translation of Red Dirt Heart 2*)

Faire Face (*French translation of Red Dirt Heart 3*)

Trouver sa Place (*French translation of Red Dirt Heart 4*)

Rote Erde (*German translation of Red Dirt Heart*)

Rote Erde 2 (*German translation of Red Dirt Heart 2*)

PRIVATE
Charter

N. R. WALKER